I0608167

BY FLESH ALONE

Also by March Hastings

Abnormal Wife
Again and Again
The Boys of Brigham Dee
By Flesh Alone
Crack-Up
The Demands of the Flesh
Design for Debauchery
Enraptured
Fear of Incest
The Heat of the Day
Her Private Hell
The Jealous and Free
Obsessed
The Outcasts
A Rage Within
Savage Surrender
The Soft Way
Three Women
The Third Sex
The Third Theme
The Unashamed
Veil of Torment
Whip of Desire

BY FLESH ALONE

MARCH HASTINGS

CUTTING EDGE

Copyright © 1962 by March Hastings

The characters and events portrayed in this book are fictitious. Any similarity to real persons, living or dead, is coincidental and not intended by the author. No part of this book may be reproduced, or stored in a retrieval system, or transmitted in any form or by any means, electronic, mechanical, photocopying, recording, or otherwise, without express written permission of the publisher.

ISBN-13: 978-1-952138-89-8

Published by
Cutting Edge Books
PO Box 8212
Calabasas, CA 91372
www.cuttingedgebooks.com

CHAPTER ONE

"SOMEDAY, Danny, you're going to love me the way I loved you all these years," she said. "But when that time comes, don't tap me on the shoulder. Because I'll turn around and spit in your face."

Rain slobbered in from a crooked window. It drove a grim tattoo against the rattly panes, goading her on like a drum beat.

The wall mirror reflected Lila's image back to herself. She saw this thing she had become—hate alloyed with iron—heft a suitcase.

It could have been good between us.... We had two such wonderful years.... Why did you stop loving me, Danny?... Why?

The brick wall of Danny's back curved slightly over his desk. She studied the profile of him outlined by the corduroy drape. A twinge of memory, of desire still glowing, shook her tight body. But only for a moment. Then the envelope of ice, a merciful protective coating, rolled up along her skin. The suitcase swung from her icy fingers. It felt surprisingly light against the strength of her determination.

"Did you find a place?" Danny said, his voice very soft, so different from the temper storms. So patient and caring, now, when it could no longer matter.

"I have friends, you know." Her stubborn mouth clipped the words. "You need friends, Danny. Find them."

He closed the book of crossword puzzles and slipped a stub of pencil behind his ear. "You know what I need," he answered with a hint of challenge.

She couldn't take it. Not now. The petals of him opening toward her, still hoping she might change her mind.

"Well, get yourself a maid, anyway," Lila said, softening a little. "Before the dust piles up to your knees."

He tossed the book of puzzles onto the scattering of butts in the fireplace. "I'll get myself another wife," he said matter-of-factly.

His words hit her low in the stomach. The dismal, cold rain seemed to pour through her. "Yes, do that," she said. "One who'll adore you and not ask questions."

Because she was trembling, because he seemed so far away and yet so touchable, Lila drove herself out the door.

She paused beneath the canopy, blinking to right and left for signs of a cab. It was almost five and taxies were busy with rush hour. Behind her, the expensive building loomed like a threatening taint of yesterday's bad dream. She could not stand here, helpless and lost. One thing Danny had taught her: make decisions fast and change them slowly. She sailed off into the sheets of water, intent on catching a bus, anything that would put distance between them.

On Seventy-ninth Street, two buses waited, empty at the end of their run. She climbed up into the damp, rubbery smell of the first one, found change and pushed the valise through the aisle until she reached the back seat.

Her body collapsed on the green leather with a sigh. Her thighs felt moist where the thin skirt of her suit clung. She moved her calves close to where heat drifted out from beneath a seat.

Patience … patience.

The idling bus seemed to mock her, reminding Lila how long it might take before the flavor of Danny would dissolve completely from her being.

She jostled westward, then downtown along Fifth Avenue, watching the bus crowd with alien faces. A man, his hat brim dripping water, shot her a grim look as he climbed over the valise. Lila's body tightened away from him. She felt like a tiny shell rolling on a windswept beach—small, helpless, worn. And this strangeness of riding alone prodded her to realize how narrowly she had lived during the long years with Danny.

She pushed aside damp bangs plastered to her forehead and stared back brazenly at the crowd jamming around her. She had a lot to make up for, a lot of living to do. And now, Lila told herself, was the time to get started.

The bus circled through Washington Square. She got off near the playground and hurried away from the squealing, empty swings banging in the wind.

In a few minutes, she had reached her destination, her feet moving automatically, without signals from her brain.

Marge's house sagged tiredly behind a row of garbage cans.

Lila pushed into the narrow hallway, striding through an odor of stale fish. The wooden steps held her weight dubiously as she climbed the six flights. It was the house she had run from … to Danny … many years ago. Away from the spaghetti and beer dinners, the endless circle of women, of men, drifting in to stay for the night. But now she felt glad, glad to stretch herself once more toward the pot-luck style of Marge's life.

At the very best, she might stumble into a new future. At the worst, it would be a change from Danny's slow strangulation.

Lila rapped at the splintery door.

Her small lips began to smile expectantly as she heard the creaking sound of footsteps coming to answer.

"Well, girl," Marge said, standing back to let Lila in, "what's this?"

"I've left him." She set her bag down beneath the hems of coats hanging from hooks in the hall foyer.

Marge's thin face tossed back its heavy weight of lank hair. "You what?" Her large, starved eyes widened.

"We've separated by mutual agreement," Lila said stiffly, as though the formal, rational tone could make sense where there had been no sense for so long.

"Permanently?"

Lila watched the anxious, bony hands hook into the wide belt of dungarees. "I think so," she said softly, unable to look up into Marge's face.

Suddenly Marge threw her long arms high. "Wheeeee!"

It was a banshee cry of relief. The rebels had won. The underdog had turned over the stone and crept out into the sunlight.

In a way, Marge's glee made Lila proud. But it was a hollow pride that rang tinnily. She stepped around the rivulets running from the four corners of the valise and pushed through the clutter of second hand furniture, the scatter of books and pages scribbled with poetry to the two-burner stove.

"Got some coffee for an old friend?" she asked in a shaky voice.

"Coffee. Anything you want," Marge answered, glowing. "Just get out of those wet clothes."

Lila did as she was told. She liked being told things. Only it had to be in a way she needed to hear. Compliments, encouragement, acceptance. Not the continual fire of Danny's criticism that had ripped her wide.

"Just relax," Marge soothed, pouring coffee and milk. "Don't you worry about a thing."

"Why not?" Lila asked honestly.

"Look," Marge said, coming to sit beside her, "we used to be good friends, didn't we? Didn't we have fun together? Didn't we used to be two nuts together and love it?"

"Yes," Lila agreed, wanting to be part of Marge again, forcing herself to believe that this was right, that this was good.

"We can have the same good times again," Marge murmured, "now that you've come to your senses."

Lila felt fingers stroking her shoulder. Oh, yes, they had been friends. They had flown kites together and gathered sea shells in the sun, sat quietly on Christmas Eve making a tree out of coat hangers and construction paper. And best of all, they had known how to share silences.

Marge was silent now. Only her dark, secret eyes glowed like a fireplace, warming Lila.

The hand moved down from her shoulder to her arm. And from her arm to the side of her breast.

"Don't," Lila whispered.

But Marge, intent now, earnest, seemed not to hear.

"You'll stay here as long as you like," she whispered against Lila's throat.

Lila balanced between desire and truth. The days of being attracted to Marge were long gone by. Yet the warmth, the acceptance, the wanting hovered around her. She knew Marge still found her desirable. And she herself needed someone to fill in all the empty spaces in her soul ... spaces reserved for Danny, yet spaces he had never filled.

Without wanting to, Lila let herself lean in closer to the girl. Their knees touched. Marge found her hand and held it, quietly rubbing the place where her wedding ring had been. Rubbing off the dent of it in her flesh.

Lila rested her chin on Marge's shoulder. She watched the whirling twist of rain writhing in the courtyard. Beneath her, the old sofa felt warm. And Marge's thin body felt warm. Almost breathless, it pressed in close to Lila's full bosom.

The years of Danny turning away from her in the night welled up to choke her. Swollen with desire, with a kind of numb grief, Lila could not pull away. Her arms encircled Marge's waist like vines needing a tree to grow around. She drew the pulsing body tight to her own. Their lips, their breasts, their flat bellies met, mingling and stirring desire. In the damp little apartment, they could burn hot, flaming up to scare away the demons of the night.

"I want you," Lila said, surrendering to the turmoil of her passion.

Her hands slipped upward to cup Marge's head and Marge stretched beneath her, drawing Lila down, full length on the couch.

She slipped Marge's shirt free and put her head beneath it, searching upward and across, tasting one breast, tasting the other, sensing the little prickles of thrill driving Marge's lean flesh into shuddering hardness. This, Lila could share. Her own breasts pushed against the cups of her brassiere and she waited while Marge unfastened the hooks.

They wiggled free of their clothes. Naked now, they lay rubbing gently against each other, slipping in the first film of their sweat.

Marge knew how.

Marge appreciated.

Marge wanted her as Lila had not been wanted for longer than she could remember.

Or so Lila chose to believe, as her face moved wildly along the gaunt lines of this body reaching to possess her.

Her brain seemed to split open like a coconut hitting cement, releasing the tightly controlled energies, the stifled desperation, the silent cry for love that Danny had never answered.

She drove herself against Marge, working at the girl's body with sudden, angry need, killing Danny with every thrust of her body, spilling the liquid love that had been stored for too long.

CHAPTER TWO

AFTERWARD, they talked.

Not about Danny or anything important...

Just talk to fill in time...

And Marge cooked corned beef hash with a fried egg on top. They ate placidly, now that talk had run out. Lila felt some of the resentment toward Danny that she had thrived on begin to dilute and wash away.

"I need to find a place of my own," Lila said, sipping wine from a chipped crystal stem glass. "Something cheap, like this."

"So soon?" Marge said, studying the colors in her own glass and frowning between the long ears of her hair.

"Soon as possible."

It was the one way of telling Marge that what had happened between them must not go on. With passion calmed, she had begun to think a little bit. And thinking meant the return of her determination.

"I've got to do something important for myself," Lila mused, speaking more to herself than to Marge.

"It's the only life you've got," Marge smiled, settling herself among her belongings. "That's for sure. So what would you like to do with it?"

The question touched Lila in the sensitive tissues of the promise she had once made to herself, long ago; long before Danny for whom she had thrown it all over. "Architecture," she said quietly.

"Well, that's a sturdy profession," Marge said with respect. "You'll have to go to school, though, won't you?"

Lila nodded, smiling to herself at Marge's awe. "I used to be good at school. Good at everything, in fact, until I came to New York." She picked out two walnuts and cracked them one against the other, feeling with satisfaction the strength in her hands, the patiently waiting strength that would mold her into a person.

"New York isn't so bad," Marge said, taking a lumpy, home rolled cigarette from a Swedish pencil box. "In fact, you picked a good night. I'm expecting a couple of people in to look at my poems. Maybe publish a few." She twisted her pale lips into a wry smile. "One of them, name of Jingle, always has apartments on tap. Maybe he can even fix you up at Cooper Union."

Lila surveyed the tangled forest of Marge's prospects for her. Marge always had an escape hatch She had come to her, really, knowing that the girl knew people. Helpful people. Someone to get her poems published. Someone to do the heavy work in building a cabinet. Someone to borrow a car from. Lila knew she could put herself safely in Marge's hands and get all the dirty work done for her like magic.

The thought tasted good. It also tasted bitter, like the bit of shell in a walnut that had mixed in with the meat. Yet she had leaned too long on Danny to consider herself independent now. Self-reliance took time, work ... and most of all, it took desire.

"There they are now." Marge's head quirked toward a knock at the door. "And don't worry. They're my friends."

Lila stirred sugar into her coffee as Marge went to the door. She watched the tight, boy-shaped behind stride long legs and considered how pleasant it felt to be with someone who always said the right things, the precious, encouraging things.

Now a babble of conversation flooded out the intimacy she had shared with Marge. Lila straightened herself and crossed her legs. She slipped her fingers quickly through her short hair, smoothing it down around the curve of her skull. Her lips felt dry. The button down shirt and tight pants she had borrowed from

Marge looked just a trifle too rumpled. Suddenly she wished that Marge had given her earlier warning of company.

The pair who entered looked like espresso drinkers she had known years ago when coffee houses were far-out and romantic.

"Lila, this is Carmen Quayle and Jingle Taylor."

Carmen couldn't unglue her mild blue gaze from Marge, but Jingle shoved one cold, wet hand out to grasp Lila's as he shrugged out of the bulky, stained trench coat.

"Hi, cat," he said, his rusty beard bobbing.

Lila, eager to be sociable, felt something wrench away in disdain. Perhaps it was Carmen's little piggy face, so openly adoring, or her round, swollen behind offered to the world in all its glory beneath strained stretch pants. Or perhaps it was Jingle's large teeth, a little too yellow and pitted as though in the process of becoming Swiss cheese.

But she snapped off the feelings almost before she knew them and nodded hello to them while Marge continued the linty conversation that covered them all like dog hairs.

"Do you write poetry too?" Jingle said, flopping down beside Lila and pulling up the lost crease from his tweed pants.

"Nope," Lila said, feeling oddly jaunty. "Only post cards."

"Lila's mainly visual," Marge intruded.

"I can see that," Jingle flipped back, his gaze circling the nest of her bosom.

Lila pushed herself deeper into the cushions. His remark was part of the game. A stupid game she had been sheltered from by Danny. But now, it was out in the open and she had to learn to cope with it again. So she waited while Jingle took his fill and watched Carmen meanwhile, sitting herself gingerly on a hassock and folding her hands sacredly on her fat thighs while she blinked up at the god that was Marge. Lila lit another cigarette while Marge poured coffee for all. Smoking veiled the contempt she felt for Carmen. And the envy, too, for it had been a very long time since she had adored a creature of flesh and blood.

"So," Jingle said, snapping a cracker in half, "will you read for us?"

Marge had been waiting. Now she played casual. "You haven't caught your breath yet from the stairs."

"Marge, please do," Carmen breathed.

Lila felt oddly surprised that the girl could speak. But it wasn't at all surprising that Marge should keep her around as a foil, so that she herself might appear modest.

The appeal in Carmen's tone seemed to convince Marge that she had no choice. She scrambled among a pile of papers on a flush door propped on filing cabinets to make a desk.

> *I have nose and eyes*
> *and earrings,*
> *I have kisses young*
> *and sweet,*
> *I have nights all filled*
> *with dreamings,*
> *I have blisters on my feet...*

Slyly, Lila peeped at the reception of Marge's inept sincerity. Jingle crossed and recrossed his legs while Marge's voice rolled on. Cigarette smoke rolled past Carmen's eyes and she seemed to be gazing through a great misty veil on the Mount of Olives, her thick pink ears attuned to the low, musical voice, while her brain cared nothing about the words.

Lila wished it would finish soon. She pulled deep into herself and considered the practical matter of apartment hunting while Marge concluded.

Jingle said, "You're a primitive, Marge. We'll make room for you in the summer issue."

His glance darted restlessly over the shelves.

"Wine?" Marge said as though reading him intuitively. Her pale cheeks flushed slightly with gratitude for Jingle's acceptance.

Here we go again, Lila thought, watching the bottle tilting over glasses.

A small eddy of loneliness began to swirl inside her. She needed a drink now. Needed to make herself a part of things. And she gave herself to the Chianti as she had given herself to Marge.

Time and night began to dissolve. A small bulb went on behind her brain, lighting the apartment with a friendly glow. When Jingle toppled against her, she tried to push him away. But her arms felt heavy, all of her sluggish.

"What the hell?" Lila murmured as Jingle's head slipped into her lap.

"You're a funny girl," Jingle said with his eyes closed.

"How?"

"That face of yours. I can't tell what's going on behind it."

"Nothing," Lila laughed. "Nothing at all."

Fuzzily, she blinked across to Marge, expecting her to do something about the bearded lump of face rolling around on her thighs. But Marge was sitting now on the hassock beside Carmen. She did not see Lila's plea.

"I guess I'm on my own with you," Lila breathed, words bubbling up recklessly. "What good are you going to do me?"

Jingle wiped his tongue over his teeth. "Whatever you need, baby, I got it waiting for you."

"I need a place to live. Got that waiting for me?" She felt a little wild, unhappily pleasant. One leg had fallen asleep and her toes tingled.

"Want to go now?" Jingle murmured. "I got a nice loft. Real cozy."

"Yours? Or for rent?"

"Don't be difficult."

"I'm difficult by nature."

"Go with him, Lila," Marge intruded. "What have you got to lose?"

Marge was right. What had she to lose, indeed? Neither her heart nor her virginity. A strange, solid imperviousness had taken over. She could crawl through the great daisy chain that encircled the world and not feel a thing where it counted.

"Okay," she said, "I'm game."

She lifted Jingle's head and slid from the couch. The room stank like a chicken coop from all the stale smoke. A great yearning in her lungs screamed for air. She must walk in the rain. Soak herself thoroughly through. Maybe with a little luck and with lots of practice, she could learn again to live as Marge lived—for the moment. But now...

"Take my raincoat," Marge called after her.

Lila caught a faint tone of relief in Marge's voice. She sensed that Marge was glad to get rid of her just now. Lord only knew why, but Marge wanted to be alone with Carmen. She glanced at the pair and saw Marge flirting her way toward the girl's inviting body.

Cynically, it snapped into Lila's brain that the girl must have cash.

The sight of the two of them turned something sour far back on Lila's tongue. She didn't want Marge's raincoat now. Didn't want to see her again. Not for a long, long time.

Hurrying to the hallway, she snapped open her valise and pulled out a weatherproof jacket.

Then she trotted down the stairs, all of her running from Marge, fleeing from the breezy, sporting poetical life that was really nothing more than empty greed.

Lila lifted her face to the steady rain. It chopped against her eyelids, dribbled into her mouth, slid along her throat to soak into her opened collar. A little seed seemed to burst wide open inside her. She stretched out her arms and laughed at the sky.

"What's so funny?" Jingle said.

"I am," Lila whispered to the heavens. "Don't you know yet just how funny I am?"

Jingle grabbed her wrist and pulled her through the streets.

She was drunk, dead drunk, and she didn't care.

She had not been this drunk for years and it took possession of her body.

"Let's have fun," she called to Jingle, tripping up onto the curb. "Lots and lots of fun."

"Baby, that's what I'm made for," Jingle said.

CHAPTER THREE

THEY did the bars.

Lila swam through them, meeting faces, hearing names, her world murky and cold like the bottom of a vast sea. Strangers kissed her neck, shook her hand, filled up her glass. She heard herself making promises, agreeing to appointments, laughing into earlobes. Someone danced with her and she felt him pressing into her. She stumbled through a doorway and puked, scattering a family of indignant cats.

Another glass…Ice cubes jingling…Brubeck jazz weaving rhythms…Neons blinking green…Her eyelids burned. Her stomach felt torn across the middle. A piece of spongy cake tasting of garlic…or was it rum?…The back seat of somebody's car…A hand along her thigh. Her own hand searching…Her limbs entwined with his…Two bodies straining, becoming one. Fun…fun…

Lila awoke to the metal jarring of springs against one shoulder blade. She turned on the cot and struggled to pull open her pasted eyelids. Her tongue, swollen and cracked, filled all of her mouth. She swallowed painfully and managed to sit up.

The long room filled with unframed paintings smelled of raw turpentine. She rubbed her cheeks with the heel of either hand and blinked at a shaft of sunlight glistening from two tall windows. There was no furniture in the room except this puzzle of rusted springs beneath her and a gas heater in the middle of the naked floor.

Her stomach felt as though a herd of giraffes had thundered through.

"Morning, fuzzy head," a male voice called. His face peered around a partition. "I'm making bacon if you want some."

"No, thanks," Lila groaned. "Just coffee. Gallons of it."

She had to struggle to find the name that belonged to the face.

He came to her with a steaming mug. "Here you go, girl."

Lila's fingers reached for the handle but they shook so that she paused. "Better put it on the floor," she said.

"That's a dilly of a hangover."

"What day is this?" Lila said.

"Wednesday. Why? You got a date?"

She wanted to laugh in his face. Wednesday.... Then she'd been on this binge since Monday evening. She tried lifting the cup. Maybe, with a steadied head, Tuesday would return to tell her what she'd been doing.

"You're a wild one, all right," Jingle said, sitting down on the floor beside her and crossing his legs. "How come you're not a poet?"

"What are you," Lila smiled, "a publisher or a missionary?"

"Just a guy."

"Well, I'm just a gal. Little Miss Bo Peep, to you."

"Looking for the sheep?"

"Exactly."

She still had on the dungarees and they stuck to her stiffly. "Look, Jingle, you got a bathtub, by any slim chance?"

Jingle pointed to the ceiling. "The Katzes upstairs built in a shower."

"Don't bother," she sighed as he started to get up. "I'll use the sink, if you don't mind."

"Help yourself."

She knew that Jingle would give her no privacy. One couldn't expect privacy while living the poet's life. Comforts, solitude, a chance to pull the mess of yourself together was reserved for the middle classes. The Dannys of the world.

Doggedly she went to the sink, took off her shirt and the sweated bra beneath. Her breasts cascaded to the porcelain, sore with handling, sore with an odd neglect that came from too much attentiveness. Slowly, she lathered herself, wondering who Danny was using for consolation.

"I hate to bring this up," Jingle said from where he sat on the windowsill. "But does the sport have any green stuff for groceries?"

Lila draped a dirty towel across her breasts and wiped them slowly. "I'll make a deal with you," she said blandly. "You rent me this place, to live in alone, and I'll pay you three months rent in advance. Plus commission."

Jingle pulled his knees up to his chin. "A rich fish, eh?"

"Yes or no?" Lila persisted with a hard-headed certainty that Jingle could not turn down such an offer.

"I need a place to sleep too, you know."

"You've got plenty of places."

Carefully she fastened her brassiere behind her back. "A hundred bucks commission," she goaded. "I'd have to pay as much to an agent anyway. So why not to you?" The offer, she knew, was irresistible. "And you can leave the paintings."

"They aren't mine," Jingle said, gazing down to the street one floor below them. "This place isn't mine either," he added regretfully. "But you can stay here till the girl gets back. Maybe longer."

"Good."

Lila tucked her shirt tail in and went back to the coffee. "Now why don't you be a good little boy and go?" She strode toward him and thrust a twenty dollar bill into his hand. "This settle it?"

Jingle grabbed the bill. "I really hate to take this."

"Force yourself," Lila smiled as he stuffed it into his pocket.

She spent the next ten minutes edging him out of the apartment.

And when he closed the door between them, Lila knew that she hadn't seen the last of him yet. Like Marge, he had a sure instinct about money. And she had a nice backlog of capital in the bank. Her own savings plus Danny's allowance.

As she took inventory of the place, a rumbling above her head told Lila that the Katzes had children who liked to roller skate. She smiled. Family living seemed like a cry of shame, admonishing her with its good will, its teamwork, its essential contentment.

It occurred to her that maybe the Katzes would be friendly. If they let Jingle use their shower, they must be.

Quickly she combed her hair, put on lipstick and climbed the stairs, eager to introduce herself, to find a single strand of sanity running through the mess of her existence.

Red letters painted on the black door spelled out Isaac and Minnie Katz. Beneath, in brighter letters, as though added nine months later, Allen Paul Katz.

Lila knocked.

The rumbling of skates squealed as though in a circle, then rushed toward the door.

A small freckled face, smeared sticky, looked up at her from beneath a black cowboy hat.

"Hi," the boy said. "Momma's in the bathroom."

"That's all right. Are you Allen?"

He took in a deep breath and held it. "No. I'm Georgie."

She smiled, playing the game with him. "Well, Georgie, my name is Lila. May I come in and wait for your mother?"

"Sure."

He skated away from her and around plasterboard partitions that carved the big loft into three small rooms. A faintly salty odor of fried herring tingled in the air. Lila padded over the throw rugs and sat down into a wooden rocker that faced a wall of gleaming appliances. The washing machine hummed, spinning clothes behind its window like a television set gone crazy.

"I don't know you," Georgie said, belly whopping over the arm of a love seat and kicking his legs in the air.

"We're neighbors now," Lila explained, watching his thick lashes flutter with a sudden nervousness. "I live right below you."

"In Waldo's house? How come?"

Waldo? A funny name for a girl, Lila thought. And she smiled to herself, envisioning the girl that would go with the name.

Heavy footsteps flapping house shoes interrupted her thoughts. The door opened to display Minnie Katz resplendent in the door frame. Coils of white blonde braids encircled her head and beneath it, milky white skin billowed out in puffs of fat.

Lila realized that beneath the rolls, Minnie had much to offer. The woman handled her surprise at finding a stranger in her house by smiling with welcome.

Lila explained her presence and started to get up.

"Sit, sit," Minnie said, flipping one wrist. "You don't need to tell me. That *meshuggeneh* Waldo runs everybody crazy. How many times the girls come up here to sit and rest a while from her shenanigans. Allen, stop swinging and sit like a *mensch*."

"I'm Georgie," the boy said solemnly, pulling his hat down over his ears. "So I don't have to listen to you."

Minnie sighed patiently. She was not yet past twenty five, yet she seemed old with the old fashionedness of eternity. "Take it from me, Lila, children have brains that make you stop to think."

"I've never met Waldo," Lila said. "I'm living downstairs alone."

"God bless you," Minnie said as she poured boiling water from a tin pot into two cups. "You don't know what you missed."

"Me, too," the boy said as Minnie put the cups on a flowered table cloth.

"Take off the skates first."

"They're not skates," the boy said mysteriously. "They're skis."

"Whatever they are, take them off already. You give Lila a headache skating over her head up and down, up and down."

Minnie sounded strained though her chins jiggled pleasantly as she spoke. Lila realized that there was little understanding between this woman and her child.

"You can't take off skis when it's snowing," he protested, skating to the table.

"The sun is shining, Allen. Take off the skates already." She settled herself like a brooding hen opposite Lila. "I can't let him down the street alone. He gets into fights with the big kids and I never know how he's coming home. I thank God he's in the school mornings."

Lila sipped her tea while Allen hovered enviously.

"Is it hot?" he said, peering over her shoulder.

"Tell you what," Lila said. "When the snow stops and you can go without your skis, why don't you come downstairs to me and we'll drink tea in the Swiss castle?"

She saw Allen's eyes relax slightly as he let out a bit of air from his thin chest.

"Say thank you to the nice lady." Then, turning to Lila as Allen scooted evasively behind her chair, she said, "Even my husband can't handle him. And Isaac's not a person you can fool so easy."

"I don't want to take up your whole day," Lila said, knowing beforehand what Isaac would be like. Minnie the easy going, Isaac the strap wielder. And Allen caught in the middle.

"Soon as the snow stops," Allen called after her with secret glee as she left the apartment.

Downstairs, alone in the loft with its weird, twisted paintings, Lila felt the first onslaught of desolation.

This will never do, she told herself, fighting off the disappointment of Marge, the disgust with Jingle and the sharp criticism of herself. It seemed that nobody in the world was happy. Not even Minnie Katz. Not really. And she could well understand why Allen would rather be Georgie skiing in the Alps than living a dismal life on Avenue A.

Minnie's tea was sparring with Jingle's coffee and Lila knew that before she did anything else, she must go out to a drugstore for an Alka Seltzer.

She leaned out the window to discover a warm day stirring up soot and colored with pyramids of grapefruits and oranges on pushcarts wheeling behind traffic.

In a minute, she was out on the street, mingling with shoppers and loiterers, searching it seemed for the needle of herself in this great pile of straw called humanity.

Some blocks away, she found a dirty candy store where she got the Alka Seltzer and a lemon ice to carry along while she strolled the sidewalks.

Thoughts of Tuesday, forever lost, plagued her. She hated the helplessness of not knowing, of running into people with whom she might have slept … and not even knowing their names.

Slowly, she ambled westward to Washington Square Park where students from the university clustered on benches. She saw their books piled beside them. It prodded her to remember her own ambitions. But ideas of school seemed out of step with her today. She needed organization, a pattern of living. How could she dare pretend she had found this while camping in Waldo's apartment. Waldo, the *meshuggeneh,* as Minnie said. Lila smiled at the firmness of Minnie's convictions. But Minnie, at least, had sorted out right from wrong, something like the red and black squares on a checkerboard.

The lemon sweetness was turning acid in her mouth and she sauntered along the path to a water fountain, crowded round with sweaty children.

And when she turned around, there on a bench, in cotton walking shorts with the *Times* folded lengthwise, sat Danny.

He appeared not to see her but she could not be certain. One dark curl of hair tousled to his forehead and he hunched sideways, obviously engrossed in his reading.

Lila started the other way, hurrying to get out of sight before he looked up. She raced across the street, skidding in front of the bumper of a moving car, and disappeared down the block to the sound of curses flung at her by the driver. Her heart thudded wildly, taking away breath. Danny didn't like the Village. Always made nasty remarks about the inhabitants and about her old way of life.

So what was he doing here now?

And why, for heaven's sake, reading a paper in the park?

It made no sense to her. But she knew one thing clearly. She must not meet with him, talk with him. Not for a long, long while. Not until all the jigsaw pieces of herself were fitted into place. She could not face Danny's calm while she was off-balance herself. For he would see her vacillation. Make fun of it. Assume that she wanted to come home, but couldn't give in because of pride.

But that wasn't true.

While she leaned against the window of a hardware store to catch her breath, she told herself firmly that going back to Danny was the last thing in this world she wanted.

For it would start again. The squabbles, the contempt, the resentment. No more Danny. No more turmoil. Peaceful living. A career. In time, perhaps, another love.

But no Danny.

Definitely, no Danny.

And while she thought this, he might be coming around the corner. She felt herself exposed to the bright light of day with no hole to jump into. No rabbit hole for the rabbit.

Blindly, but with the pressure of her resolve, Lila found a movie house and entered its cool, protective dark.

She climbed to the balcony and snuggled down low in a plush seat. She could watch all the other empty seats, lighted just enough by the yellow side bulbs to give her warning in case he too might wander in.

The picture reeled off, wide and colorful and romantic. She watched it while her ears buzzed noisily with the more immediate complications of her own story. A dull pain in her throat struggled to squelch the terror of her unexpected encounter. Her skin felt like dry, crumbling flakes of an old house slowly going to rot.

She could not deny, after all, that she still loved him. Loved him, in spite of everything. Loved him with one stubborn half of her, while the other struggled just as stubbornly to create a new life.

For loving him meant more than pain. It meant death. A death of the heart, slowly but sure. There had been times during the past year when she had considered jumping out the window as her only escape.

So, though she loved him, she must not let it dominate her. She must find, with time, another love, stronger, more engulfing and harmonious so that the music of it would drown out all the discordant feelings toward Danny.

The picture droned on. It ended. Then music. The theater lights came up. Off again. Some young men shuffled into the first row and put their feet on the railing. Another picture started. She wondered if the sun had gone down yet, if Danny had finished his paper and gone home. She cursed the leave he had taken from teaching to finish his doctorate. For now he had no obligations. No routine that she could count on to keep him safely away from her.

And the movie circled round again to the first film. She sat a while, her eyes burning with the strain. One side of her behind had gone numb. A calf muscle throbbed. She fiddled with her bangs and decided that what she needed was a haircut.

At last, because she could not stay trapped there forever, Lila got up and went downstairs to the ladies' room.

She splashed cold water on her face, goading it to come alive. The fluorescent lighting splotched her cheeks with an unbecoming purple. The wrinkles around her eyes wrote their commentary on the past few days she had lived through. Her nose looked somewhat sharper, pinched with tension. In the beginning she had thrived on the one compliment Danny had permitted himself to give her. But she saw no beauty now in the sharpened cheek bones and the tightened bow of her mouth. If anything, she looked like an old crone. A bitter old apple seller, floating with the dregs on Broadway.

Well, tomorrow would be different. Tomorrow, breakfast at breakfast time. Some new clothes. Self-encouragement.

Lean on no one, Lila, Danny had taught her. *Because you'll only slip off and fall on your face.*

CHAPTER FOUR

SHE forced herself to walk home keeping her eyes straight ahead. In case Danny were still around, she would not see him.

Street lamps had come on and the sidewalks were crowded with the first spring flush of tourists. Clean shaven men, women in expensive dresses, people from the suburbs—all slumming. She felt eyes searching after her, trying to decide if she were a bohemian, a queer or something.

How silly it all felt. And how futile. For one day, she must look right back. Without looking, one would never find the right face, the special pair of eyes that might lead one to fall in love again.

She pushed her way along Eighth Street past huddles of girls at shop windows and gangs of swishes just shopping the streets. Determinedly, she swung along, her goal focused on the quiet blocks stretching beyond the other side of University Place.

When she reached the dark, quiet side street, Lila sighed as though saved from lurking hooks.

A drunk rolled from a doorway. The acrid smell of urine rose from him. She hurried past, then paused and turned to make sure that it wasn't a dead man or someone who needed help. She heard him snore then and went on, glad of the prospect of a bed she could sleep on alone. And unmolested.

She climbed the single flight and pushed open the warped door.

"Well, honey, who are you?"

The woman in pants streaked with paint got up from the gas heater that she had taken apart. Her smile was warm, soft, welcoming… like a caress somehow, Lila thought. She could not look steadily into that face because its mild gray eyes seemed to search right through to her.

"Lila Brogan," she said, turning for something to do and finding the sloppy cot to straighten.

"I'm Waldo who lives here," the girl said, still fiddling with the heater.

"Yes, I know."

"Minnie?"

"Um hmm."

"Minnie says I'm *meshuggah*."

"I know that, too."

They both laughed. A lovely sound of notes tuned in pitch with each other.

"If you'll stop fussing with that sheet, I'll give up on this heater," Waldo said, struggling up from the plethora of parts.

"Well, just let me finish," Lila insisted, not yet sure of what the expression on her face might reveal. "We need some place to sit."

"We can sit in a coffee shop," Waldo said. "I haven't eaten all day."

"Neither have I," Lila remembered.

"Well, then?"

"All right."

Lila felt an urge to comb her hair. She had just fixed it in the movies, yet somehow it felt all messed up again. But there was no mirror in the room. Waldo wasn't the kind who used mirrors.

Out of the corner of her eye, Lila watched Waldo getting to her feet. She moved smoothly, as though she swam a lot. Her short, reddish hair seemed tousled just right for the tanned face clean of make-up.

"We weren't expecting you for six weeks," Lila explained. The desire for sleep had suddenly vanished. She felt alive and bright. A feeling she had not known for too long.

"Who's we?" Waldo said, holding the door open.

"Jingle. He rented me your place because you'd be gone for that long."

"Rented? The lousy bum. He knew I'd be back by this weekend. A show is coming up and I have to get my stuff organized."

They were out on the street again. Yet it was suddenly a street that Lila had never walked before. Everyone, somehow, had lost their grim expressions. They looked happy, enjoying life, good health and the balmy weather. And she realized that she too was smiling.

"I didn't bring in clothes or anything," Lila said. "I can take a furnished room tonight."

Waldo walked on the outside, striding with hands in pockets. She looked only half civilized with her faded tee shirt flopping outside the belt of tight trousers. "Don't fret," she said gently. "Stay for the night. I'll shack up with a pal."

"But it's your place," Lila argued. "You're entitled."

Waldo shrugged. "Let me display my smattering of manners, will you?"

They looked into several coffee houses on McDougal Street and finally discovered a table for two in one on Bleecker.

Lila felt glad that they were sitting beside the large glass window. It gave her something to look at, people to glance off to if she found it impossible to look at Waldo too long.

They ordered iced cappucino and sandwiches of Italian salami. Waldo ate like a demon, devouring three more sandwiches like it before pausing for breath. Then she leaned back in the chair and patted her belly.

"Better?" Lila said, as though to a child.

"Much." Waldo wiped her mouth on the back of her hand. "And you? You don't look like you've touched a thing."

"I guess I wasn't as hungry as I thought," Lila said, aware of the strange wings in her stomach that took up room where the food should be. She fingered half a sandwich, pushing it around on the plate. "Here," she said impulsively, "finish this for me so the waitress doesn't think it's poisoned."

"Gladly," Waldo said with happy bluntness. She reached over and took the sandwich. "I've never seen you in the Village, have I?"

"If we'd seen each other," Lila said, "I would have remembered you."

Her intonation colored the words with something she had not expected to come through. Quickly, she lifted her cup and thrust her attention to its contents.

"It's all right," Waldo said softly. "People without feelings don't belong on their feet." She stirred more sugar into her cup. "Besides, I like you. Very much. You know how to laugh without smiling."

Lila stared off to the strollers outside, then back again at Waldo. She could not jump through the glass or hide beneath the table. So she stared steadily into the wide, almond shaped eyes and let Waldo see the first blossoms of new pleasure that had grown so quickly.

"It's all right," Waldo repeated softly. "You know that, don't you?"

"If it isn't," Lila said calmly, "I'm willing to take that chance."

CHAPTER FIVE

THEY went back to Waldo's place and sorted pictures until dawn, talking as people do who want to touch each other, but are waiting.

For Lila, this was a dream. Too miraculous, too self-saving to be believed. In one instant of time, she had leaped from futility to hope, from dismal criticism into an expanding future. All thoughts of Danny had dried up and blown away. There was only this badly lighted room and this woman, a little gauche, but carefully protective beside her. If Waldo was *meshuggeneh,* then Lila was Martha Washington.

She told Waldo of her plans for school, knowing at the same time that she would throw them all over to wash Waldo's dirty trousers and straighten the lumpy cot.

"Think I'll win something?" Waldo said, surveying the canvasses they had chosen. "Or just the booby bonus?"

Lila didn't know about painting. Perhaps something representational she might judge. But these abstract masses of color, laid on thick and crusted, must have meaning that she would learn by learning Waldo.

"At the very least," Lila said, wanting to be helpful, "you'll get a show at the Met."

"Why, thank you," Waldo said, grinning. "Too bad you're not the judge."

"But I am," Lila said, stretching her legs flush with the wooden floor. "I've been judging all night and my firm opinion is that you are a natural winner."

"Tell that to Minnie," Waldo laughed.

"I'll tell it to anyone you want," Lila said solemnly.

She felt young again and clean. If Waldo would lean across and kiss her, Lila knew she could respond with every nerve in her body. She could give of herself as though there were no yesterdays, as though this day and all their tomorrows was all there was of life.

"I'll tell you," Waldo said, stifling a yawn. "Let's go up on the roof and take a nap. The sun is too good to waste."

"Yes," Lila agreed, knowing she would have said yes if Waldo suggested that they leap off the Canal Street Bridge.

Waldo found a blanket, something torn and straggly that had once been maroon. She rolled it under one arm and led the way upstairs past Minnie's door, another two flights to a tilting spread of tar littered with dog droppings and faded cigarettes. But the rains had washed away all odor and they lay down side by side to look upward at a cloudless sky and the occasional glint of a plane.

"This is the life," Waldo said. "Far from the madding crowd. You know, I used to live in the country and all I could do was ache to get to the city. Now all I do is ache to get back to the sticks again."

"Well, why don't you go then?" Lila said. "Painters are free citizens, aren't they?"

"Nope. That's a myth for slaves in a factory so they'll have something to focus on. If you want to make a buck, you've got to be where the money grows. One show. Another show. Hustle, hustle. It's a racket like anything else, Lila."

"You seem to get along," Lila encouraged.

"After a fashion. But nothing steady, you know. Sometimes I eat like a king. Sometimes I starve."

"You have a picturesque way of putting it," Lila laughed.

Waldo rolled over onto her side, propping her head on one fist to stare down at Lila. "Believe it," she said, "just now is the first time I ever wished I had a million dollars."

"Why?"

For answer, Waldo's lips came down on hers. Not hard. Not passionate. But simply as a statement of fact. An answer that would brook no argument.

A long minute passed, winging like a gull to distant horizons.

When Waldo lifted away, Lila closed her eyes and waited. Waited for whatever this woman might want from her. Waited to give as she had never given before.

"You know I'm a pretty bad risk," Waldo said softly. "No steady job. Lousy nerves. Maybe you wouldn't like it after the first flush."

"I'll like it," Lila said. "I'll thrive on it."

"You're the one who's *meshuggah*," Waldo whispered.

But Lila heard joy in the woman's voice. And love. And the promise of loyalty that would pay tribute to them both.

"Kiss me," Lila said, "and stop talking."

She felt her body being lifted by the strong arms that smelled of sweat and turpentine. Her mouth opened beneath the pressure of Waldo's lips and her tongue darted forward to meet the passion growing between them, uniting their bodies as Waldo's body pressed hard against her.

The large body smothered her with its spreading warmth. She felt strong breasts flattening against her and the pulse of a heart that insisted. Iron thighs moved against her own. A muscle above her knee jumped and she tightened herself around Waldo's hips.

They touched and yet they were not touching. For the harsh material of clothes reminded them of civilization too near. Perhaps they should get up and go downstairs. But Lila could not move. Nor did she want to. It would happen soon enough. And for this moment, she needed to lie in Waldo's possession, bathe in the trust and the offering of love.

"Please," Waldo said softly into her ear.

And Lila felt a hand fumbling with her zipper.

She could not resist. She dared not be sensible or this dream might burst like a clown's balloon.

Lila lifted her hips to let the belt come looser. Then cool fingers slipped in to find her skin.

She opened to Waldo, draining the cornucopia of her desire, feeling it fill and fill again. There would be no end to their uniting, no end to their love.

"Tired?" Waldo said after a while, her own lips moist with perspiration.

"Just beginning," Lila smiled.

The rumpled blanket beneath them bunched uncomfortably.

"We ought to go downstairs," Waldo said. "Before the cops get us."

"Yes," Lila agreed. "Besides, I don't like one way streets."

Waldo smiled with understanding. "I thought you were innocent," she bantered.

"But not stupid," Lila flung back.

They were having a good time, Lila realized. Passion and love and fun all rolled up together. Blended, like a rare whiskey. And she needed to get drunk on this. To stay high forever.

She struggled to her feet, leaning against Waldo until a bit of strength returned.

Then, arm in arm, they went down the stairs.

"Pictures be damned," Waldo said to the canvasses and stuck out her tongue at them.

"Now, now," Lila said. "We'll worry about money later on."

She could think of nothing except love. Nothing except the giving and taking of desire. They lay within a golden egg, far from the world, from necessities. She didn't want to talk about practical matters. Not about anything, except the promises of happiness.

Glad now that she had straightened the cot, Lila fell to it, bringing Waldo with her.

"Now we can be ourselves," she whispered.

"Who're they?" Waldo whispered back.

Lila pinched her arm. Waldo, whatever else she was, was a piquant sauce. She needed to taste that sauce, to savor it, to blend herself into the mixture.

"I want to see your body," Lila said without shame.

"Only if you paint it," Waldo teased.

"I'll smear it with ink if you don't shut up and get undressed."

She reached for Waldo's tee shirt and lifted it away, revealing the soft breasts free of any support. Soft, yet firm, with strong tendons lifting them high, tanned almost to their crests, waiting to be kissed.

Lila formed her lips around them, feeling her own body whirl away into dizzying sensation. She loosened Waldo's trousers and pulled them down, revealing a spareness of hip that moved smoothly into round thighs, firm enough to grasp.

The tremendous hulk of Waldo shuddered as they came in contact. Waldo curved like a great Bridge of Sighs, protecting her from the remorseless glare of day.

"Go on," Waldo said gruffly, "you can't hurt me."

They rolled together in a great convulsion. It seemed to shake the universe and destiny right side up, with all the pieces fallen into place at last.

CHAPTER SIX

"I'LL go," Waldo said, combing her hair and feeling it with her palm. "You don't have to see her again if you don't want to."

Lila lay naked on the bed watching Waldo dress, secretly pleased that she could do it without a mirror.

"No, it isn't right," she said.

"Don't be silly. You don't think you can hurt Marge's feelings, do you?"

She saw Waldo's smirk and it jostled her. "You know Marge?"

"Who doesn't?"

Lila pulled a pillow close and hugged it. The thunder of roller skates had begun again and she knew that in Allen's world, it was still snowing.

"I don't know," Lila mused. "I rather liked to think that you…"

"…were innocent?" Waldo's laugh thundered like the skates. "Well, honey, in spirit I am. Clean as a whistle, in spirit."

She sensed that Waldo thought her naive and a purple passage of shame rolled through her. Instantly, she was off the bed and pulling on her dungarees. "No more need be said," Lila insisted. "I'm going along."

Waldo shrugged. "Suit yourself, honey."

They walked through the sunshine all the way across town, laggard and relaxed from the draining of their passion. Lila ate an ice cream, licking the chocolate covering and feeling like a kid who had chased away all the nightmares.

She could barely remember Danny. He floated somewhere beyond her fingertips. She wanted only to link her arm through Waldo's. Show the world her pride. Her gaze rested on the woman who sauntered with hands in pockets, softly whistling a fragment of melody. Her sun dried skin wrinkled slightly at the bridge of her nose. Lila sensed her abstraction and knew that Waldo was deep in thought.

"What is it?" Lila said, coming in close. She wanted to know everything, be part of Waldo's total world. Make up now, in the present, for all the years they had missed together.

Waldo shook her head as though brushing off a fly.

"Come now," Lila encouraged. "It can't be that bad."

Waldo grinned. "It isn't bad at all," she said. "Just difficult."

"What's difficult?"

Waldo took a breath. It thrust out her breasts a little, giving a rooster like appearance to her chest. "I keep thinking about that damned show and the one after it," she said.

Lila heard a note of irritation. "Well, what about it?" she said cheerily. "We've decided you've got what it takes."

"Yeah. But what it takes is something to cart those blame pictures. And that I don't have."

Lila paused, disconcerted. "How did you cart them around till now?"

Waldo's sharp face turned down to her and stared into her eyes intently. "You don't want to hear that."

Lila refused to have her good mood shaken. "Why not?"

"Because it wouldn't jibe with all that talk of innocence," Waldo answered curtly.

"I see," Lila said.

And she did see. She saw the passage of rich women through Waldo's life. Money, cars, moving vans. Whatever it took, she knew had been offered to Waldo. Lila felt suddenly cold in one small corner of her back. She sensed herself in competition with all those others. They must have had brains. And beauty, too.

Golden women. And Waldo had thrown them all over for her. But for how long, if Waldo needed ...

"Now you see?" Lila's voice lilted. "It isn't as bad as you might think."

"Why not?"

"Because ... I can get you a station wagon, if it'll do," she blurted. "Maybe not something brand new and shiny. But something that'll go, anyhow."

Impulsively, Waldo hugged her. "How about that," she breathed.

Lila watched the abstraction melt and Waldo return to her. She felt glad again and secure. "You don't ever have to worry about money," she whispered. "We'll always have enough. I promise."

"Don't be a good samaritan," Waldo's voice warned. "You might grow to hate me."

"Never," Lila said.

"That's what they all say."

"Please, darling," Lila pleaded. "Try to trust me a little. I'm not like all the others. You'll see."

How did it happen, Lila wondered, that they had begun to tangle so soon? What had she done to make Waldo edge away? Waldo's moods seemed to tremble and change like the shadows of rustling foliage. One moment, they seemed so close and the next brought wariness. But how, Lila asked herself, could she expect Waldo's moods to be steady when she never knew what to expect next? How could the girl feel secure and trusting when there was no firm earth beneath her feet? It would take patience, Lila conceded. And lots of hard work, to make Waldo relax.

And patience she had in abundance. Patience and tenacity. Having clung to Danny for so long ... Danny, who didn't love her ... how easy it was going to be to fight for Waldo who did.

They reached Marge's house and picked their way around some boys sitting on the stoop.

"If you want to wait ..." Waldo said.

"No," Lila said firmly. "I want to go up. The last time I was here was pretty dismal. It'll be nice to go upstairs and feel the contrast."

She chased after Waldo, who took the steps two at a time. A prickle of rebelliousness added energy. She wanted Marge to see the change in her life. That she was no longer a begging puppy. That she had come out on top. That she had love and vitality and something worthwhile to live for now. Not in three years. Not in some limbo of the future. But now.

Waldo rattled the doorknob.

"Maybe she's not home," Waldo said too quickly.

"She's home," Lila insisted. "She might not be awake. But she's home, believe me."

She had to be home. For Lila needed her clothes. She had to dress decently so that she could go to the bank. Withdraw a round, satisfying sum and spread it out in Waldo's lap. She had to find Waldo's smile again. Feel it spreading toward her with its warmth. Its salvation.

"Coming," a muffled voice called. A voice rather high pitched and full of sunshine.

"That's not Marge," Waldo grimaced.

"No," Lila said, smiling to herself with recognition and inevitability. "That's Carmen."

"Who?"

"Carmen Quayle."

"Never heard of her."

Lila nudged Waldo playfully. "So there," she whispered. "You really are innocent after all."

The door burst wide, revealing Carmen in a smudged and dirty pinafore. Dirt smeared up from her neck and into the flushed pimples of one cheek.

"Hi," Lila said. "Did we come at the wrong time?"

"No," Carmen beamed. "If you don't mind a little dust. I was just cleaning up a bit. Come in, please."

Lila introduced them and Waldo said, "Where's your girlfriend?" without ceremony.

"Writing," Carmen breathed with low reverence. "She's working in the kitchen while I'm putting things in order. It takes a lot of management to get everything done in the spare hours," she laughed.

"Spare hours?" Waldo chided. "I thought all of Marge's hours were spare."

"Yes, but mine aren't," she said, innocently missing Waldo's jibe. "I'm holding down three part time jobs and it doesn't really leave much time."

"That's my Marge," Waldo said with a smirk of understanding. Then louder, "Marge," she called. "Where the hell are you hiding?"

"Hey, now," Marge said in her low voice. She stood up from behind a new typewriter and grinned at Waldo. "Is that the old man herself I hear?"

Marge's pleasure was unmistakable.

Lila felt Carmen shrink a little and dissolve back into her dusting.

"That it is," Waldo said. "Back from the wars." She leaned over the wobbly books. "What're you scribbling there, pretending you're a writer?"

"What are you painting?" Marge flicked back with delight. "Pretending you're an artist? Good to see you, you big bastard."

"Yeah, I been painting like a mad fool."

"Good."

"Good for what?" Waldo grinned.

"Your lovely soul."

"Ahhh!"

Marge slipped out from the cubicle and for the first time, seemed to notice Lila. Her starved face became an etching of camouflaged evil, understanding Waldo, as Waldo had understood her.

"Happy?" Marge said, tilting her head toward Lila. Her voice seemed to say, it's later than you think.

Lila didn't answer. She wished now that she hadn't come here at all. She should have forgotten about the clothes. They didn't mean anything and they could have been replaced so easily.

"Who's happy?" Waldo interjected. "Turn off that nonsense and let's all of us go out and have some shrimp."

"Why not?" Marge said. And this time her voice seemed to echo, the girls can pay.

Lila glanced at Waldo as though she couldn't believe her ears. But Waldo wasn't watching to see how she felt. Waldo, her Waldo, had turned in Marge's presence to *Jolly Old Waldo*. Lila peeped at Carmen, feeling a quick sympathy for the girl where before she had known only contempt.

"I came for my clothes," Lila said, to tell Marge and to remind Waldo subtly of the real things they still had to do.

"They're safe," Marge said off-handedly. "Right where you left them."

"They're safe," Waldo repeated. "Who could wear that tiny size anyhow?"

You don't fight with Waldo, Lila told herself. You go along with her. You prove yourself. You let her build her own trust at her own pace. You certainly don't turn into a nag.

"I know a good place on Fifty-seventh Street," Lila said, becoming one of the crowd.

"Don't be silly, child," Marge said with a certain amusement. "We have it all right around the corner."

"The Village is self-supporting," Waldo added, "like a fiefdom."

"Very good," Marge said, raising one eyebrow with respect. "May I use that?"

"Be my guest," Waldo bowed.

Now, like some plaintive sound from the forest, came Carmen's voice from beneath Marge's desk. "I have to be at work by two-thirty," she said.

Lila glanced at her watch and saw that it was already past two. Perhaps Carmen had saved the day for them both.

"Well, go to work, then," Marge jabbed with sudden cruelty. "You need to chop off some of that blubber anyhow. Didn't you promise?"

"Yes, dear."

Lila started to object. But she clamped her jaws firmly together instead. Anything she might say could only embarrass Carmen further.

She watched Marge swallow a lump of irritation and flick a glance of triumph toward Waldo. "Let's go," Marge said conspiratorially and Lila followed the two of them, trouping nonchalantly away from Carmen's desolation.

Waldo and Marge, with their long strides, swept down the street as though they owned the world. Springily, Lila kept up with them while she worked hard to swallow down the echo of Carmen's pain reverberating inside her. After all, it was none of her business, really. Not her concern, if Carmen chose to make a fool of herself for Marge.

No, not her concern at all.

Nothing could concern her as long as she kept Waldo's love.

Waldo led the way down three steps and into a long room darkened from the sun with heavy drapes and relit with the more romantic aura of candles that flickered on each table. A record player beside the cashier's desk filled the room with the baroque movement of violins. The odor of rice pilaf tanged cozily in corners where couples dawdled in open privacy.

"Gee, it's good to be home," Waldo said, pulling out one chair for Lila and the other for Marge.

Lila accepted a large, cardboard menu. Her eye flicked instantly to the prices. Expensive. Nervously, her fingers fumbled to her wallet as she tried to remember if she had enough to cover the check. But with her anxiety came a warm touch of indulgence. Waldo, her Waldo was accustomed to such extravagances as this. They would have to have a private talk soon about budgeting.

She came up from her practical thoughts to hear Waldo speaking about the show again.

"…and I figure that while Lila is sitting for me, I can take a run up to Provincetown and make arrangements for space in Whitey's gallery for the summer."

"She'll give you half a wall anytime," Marge chuckled. "You know that."

Lila watched the shadows flickering up from Waldo's chin, carving her cheekbones into jagged triangles. "What do you mean, sit for you?" she asked casually, sipping ice water from a glass.

"Somebody's got to mind the store." Waldo rested her hand on top of Lila's. "It would be a great favor. And anyhow, it's fun."

"Yes, yes," Lila said impatiently. "But what do I have to do?"

"Nothing to it," Marge put in. "You'll be sitting on Waldo's canvas chair and watching the people go by. With your looks, you might be able to sell a few things Waldo couldn't palm off in a million years."

"True," Waldo laughed at herself. "I have a way of scaring off the customers."

"It's that uncanny head of yours," Marge said. "You ought to get yourself an agent."

Lila listened to them chatter away, most of it flying past her. She had a lot to learn about the art business. A lot to learn about Waldo's odd methods of survival.

Dinner arrived. Shrimps with curry that tasted too strong to. Lila's tongue. But she ate in silence, concentrating on all the names she had never heard before. Names of people in Waldo's life. Important people for Waldo, therefore important to her. She listened and filed bits of description as they occurred. It was going to be a hectic life, keeping up with Waldo's doings. Hectic, important, satisfying. At last, Lila told herself, she was going to be of use to somebody.

As she pushed down the shrimp, her future began to build brightly. And, she promised herself silently, she would make herself so important to Waldo that nothing, not all the rich women in the world, would ever be able to come between them.

CHAPTER SEVEN

I T was much after three when they finished dinner. Too late for the bank.

Too late for getting her plans into action.

"It's okay," Waldo soothed her as they left Marge. "We can go tomorrow, can't we? Tomorrow's another day."

"I'm just aching to get started," Lila laughed. She felt better now that they were alone again.

"All right," Waldo took her hand. "We can go cruise some of the used car lots anyhow. Don't you keep a blank check handy?"

"Of course," Lila said. It had taken Danny three months to teach her to carry spare cash and a spare check.

"Then let's go."

Before Lila could head for the subway, Waldo had hailed them a cab. She told the driver an address in Brooklyn and settled back with a fresh cigarette.

While Waldo smoked, absorbed in her own thoughts, Lila listened to the meter ticking. Dinner had nibbled away ten dollars. She had another twenty in her wallet. Ordinarily it was enough to last her for an entire week. But with Waldo and her unpredictable tastes, she hoped that it would be enough to last out the night.

The driver let them out in front of Cheap Charlie's where cars sprawled out for blocks jammed tightly together like an elephant's graveyard.

"Charlie knows me," Waldo explained, trimming through the sand lot. "We do business together a couple of times a year."

Lila didn't understand. But she filed the casual statement along with all the other bits of information waiting to be sorted. Enough, now, to trust Waldo and to work at making her happy.

"Hey, Charlie boy," Waldo called over the top of a convertible.

The big man in a checked golf cap and flapping shirt sleeves turned from another customer. He recognized her; "Be with you in a sec," he called back. "Have a look around."

Waldo nodded. "Got any preference in color?" she said to Lila and squatted to peer under the bumper of a shiny wagon that looked hardly used at all.

"That seems secondary," Lila said, surveying the curve of Waldo's behind. "Just pick something that'll last."

"Don't worry," Waldo's voice came from beside one white walled wheel. "I'm an old hand at this."

Lila relapsed into silence as she stood patiently by. There were lots of wagons lined up and some tickle of self-preservation made her wonder if Waldo might be persuaded to choose one not quite so shiny but just as reliable under the hood.

Multi-colored banners, strung high and crisscrossed over the lot, swung and slapped. They seemed to be nodding encouragement, poking and convincing Lila that she could afford to spend more than she thought.

"I kind of favor this one," Waldo said, strolling around a bottle green Buick. "How about you?"

An orange lettered sign propped against the wind shield said SPECIAL.

"Is it in good condition?" Lila said weakly while her own gaze travelled the gleaming length that extended for seeming miles. It wasn't at all her idea of a used car. She could see the payments stretching out before her, month after month.

Then Lila caught herself up with a jerk. How dared she be so mercenary when Waldo needed it for her livelihood?

Danny's influence, she realized bitterly. Danny, who always read *Consumer Reports,* who had to shop for three weeks, comparing and comparing, before he would even buy a pop-up toaster.

And Waldo wasn't like Danny, she considered with pride. Waldo was too big, too important to squeeze nickels.

"I think it's beautiful," Lila said. "Let's take it."

"Good," Waldo said.

Lila heard the approval and felt warmed. She climbed into the black leather seat and stretched her legs. She could just imagine herself seated here beside Waldo as they raced along dark roads. Oh, life was going to be beautiful. And mysterious and crammed with adventure. She yanked off the SPECIAL sign and folded it in half.

"How about that," Charlie said, coming up to Waldo now. "You picked just the one I would have chosen for you myself."

"Don't I know it," Waldo said with an edge of amusement. "Lift up the hood, will you?"

"Ah, what d'ya want to get your hands greasy for? You know me long enough. Would I sell you a clinker?"

"Lift up the hood anyway," Waldo said. "I want to make friends with the motor."

Charlie shrugged and lifted the hood.

From where she sat behind the dashboard, Lila listened to them haggle. It was none of her business, this part.

"Start the engine, will you, honey?" Waldo called.

Lila slid to the driver's seat and turned the key. She heard the engine turn over with a roar and knew that there was no other car in the world for her Waldo. Not until they got rich, anyway. Then there would be Lincolns and Cadillacs. Estates in the country. A couple of great danes to sit at Waldo's feet. A Japanese houseboy. And famous people coming from all over the world to look at Waldo's paintings.

Danny could never match this, Lila warmed. Dull little Danny doing his crossword puzzles and working out esoteric problems in math that could interest no one but himself and a couple of old, hairy professors.

She saw Waldo take out a big handkerchief and nod to Charlie as she wiped her fingers.

Lila cut the engine and listened to Waldo clinching the deal. She got out of the car and came around then, knowing that without her signature on the dotted line, Waldo's dream would be just another cloud.

Charlie led them to a tiny shack and took out all the papers.

"You're gonna have a lot of use out of that car, Miss," he said to Lila as she signed.

Lila had to believe it as she filled out her blank check for the deposit and wondered why Charlie didn't seem concerned with checking out her references and credit.

Behind her, Waldo stared through the gritty window, far from the mundane juggling of dollars and cents. Lila, seated at the desk, saw herself in the future, balancing Waldo's income between ironings and making dinners. In time she would start a mutual fund plan for the security of their old age. Lila smiled affectionately as she realized that Waldo would probably scream her head off at such trivial considerations as old age.

At last, in debt for the first time in her life, Lila pushed the chair back, satisfied that she had done the proper thing for Waldo's comfort.

"That's it, folks," Charlie said, folding the papers. "Drive it away and have yourselves a ball."

Lila chased after Waldo racing to the car.

"Tell you what," Waldo said, squeeling off into the convergence of traffic. "Let's go for a good luck spin."

"Love to," Lila breathed, sidling up to Waldo's arm. The luxury around her smelled good. It was like a trousseau, promising years of love and the gathering of abundance. She pressed one of the chrome buttons and watched the radio needle glide along the numbers. All the little gadgets seemed to smile at her as they caught bits of sunlight. How different from the sparse dashboard on Danny's old Chevrolet.

The cushioned springs lulled her as Waldo headed onto the Gowanus Parkway and down along the curving rim of New York harbor that brought them to the ocean and the windy, empty beach of Coney Island.

They parked and strolled on the boardwalk, watching the sun pour melted gold over the ocean. Wind blew stinging sand to bite into Lila's eyelids, but it couldn't kill off the crazy grin rolling lopsided across her mouth. She was bouncing on the moon, light, without gravity, spinning among the planets, tumbling through an eternity of wonderment at the private miracle that had brought her Waldo. She took Waldo's arm and drew it across her shoulders, needing to be close to convince herself that this was all really happening.

"Take me home," she whispered up at Waldo's chilled ear. "I want to be alone with you ..."

Waldo grinned down at her with understanding.

"But we are alone," she teased.

For answer, Lila kissed the underside of Waldo's chin. "Alone like this will never do," she said, "for my evil purposes."

Waldo laughed out loud. "Baby, you'll go far," she said and swung Lila around toward the car.

Evening painted the sky with long daubs of orange, pink and violet as they came back to the city. And Lila, possessive about her first present to Waldo, grimaced at some kids eying the unsullied fenders as Waldo parked.

But home again all thoughts of cars, of money, of financial entanglements drifted away.

Without coyness, free of shame, gladly, openly, Lila wafted into Waldo's arms and drew Waldo's mouth down hard to her own lips. The well of her desire seemed to know no depths. She spun off dizzily into passion, new born, stripping both of their bodies of the awkward clothing that came between them.

They stood between the paintings and Lila went onto her toes, grazing along the hard muscles of Waldo's physique.

"Oh, but you're queer," Waldo laughed softly.

"What does that mean?" Lila said breathlessly while she wiggled to make herself one with Waldo's flesh.

Waldo's large hands spread across her back and pressed her in tight. "The way you need it and need it," she whispered.

"I need you," Lila grunted with blind truth. "All of you. Always."

She didn't want to talk now. Only to give, to spread herself out for Waldo's taking. She swung one leg around Waldo's calf and bent the knee in tight. Some vague premonition... maybe Waldo's comment about going to Provincetown... touched off a faint anxiety. She had to tie Waldo to her so tight that the miles between them would be as nothing. "You need it, too," Lila whispered. "You need to be had and had and..."

She drew Waldo with her past the stacked paintings to the sagging cot, burying her mouth into the firm breasts, into each crevice and cranny of the sun-warmed skin. She wished she could climb inside Waldo, to command the heart beat and the rhythm of her breathing.

You've got to love me, Lila pleaded inside her head.

Memories of Marge and Carmen nagged, flaming her desire anxiously. Her breasts burned as Waldo nuzzled them. Burned and ached as though branded with initials that could never rub off. Her flesh seemed to melt into Waldo's, their writhing bodies inseparable.

The curve of Waldo over her sheltered her with its passionate warmth. She lifted to arc in line with the body, to transfuse her passion into Waldo's veins, to build a craving that Waldo must remember always, to haunt her with an echo never to be quieted—or quiet only when they clung as now, mutually resplendent in the golden beauty of their love making.

A rapid knocking at the door ended the quiver in Lila's hips. Her body sank, trembling and unsatisfied, to the damp sheet.

"Who's that?" she said dully to Waldo.

"Damned if I know," Waldo grunted. "Wait a minute," she called with unmasked annoyance.

They flung themselves into pants and shirts.

Barefoot, Waldo tramped to the door.

Lila didn't want to see, didn't want to know another name and face in Waldo's collection. Her stomach felt sick, glutted with all the extraneous matter of Waldo's sociabilities.

"Oh, hello," Allen's voice said. "Is Lila here? She told me to come down as soon as it stopped snowing."

"Snowing?" Waldo said. "Damn it, boy..."

"That's all right," Lila interrupted. She turned to smile at Allen. "We've got a date in the Swiss castle."

"You what?" Waldo shrilled.

"We're gonna make tea and have a party," Allen explained, skipping in and batting Waldo against one hip with a tiny fist.

"Great," Waldo said. And to Lila, "You've been a busy bee."

"Georgie and I are great friends," Lila said lightly, battening down the remains of her unsated desire.

"So enjoy yourselves," Waldo said irritably. "I got to get a licence for the show anyway."

"No. I'll go with you," Lila said quickly.

"But you've got a previous date." Waldo tightened the belt of her trousers.

A sudden anger flipped out of control. "Don't be a drag," Lila said. "We can go for the licence half an hour later, can't we?"

She stood for it while Waldo surveyed her, her eyes darkening like knuckles that would brook no argument.

"There's only one boss in every house," Waldo said finally. "And I'm going for that licence now."

"So go," Lila screamed with helplessness.

She had hardly gotten out the words when the door banged, leaving a gap of misunderstanding to wash coldly between herself and the quick temper of this person she was struggling so hard to understand.

"Waldo is a *meshuggeneh*," Allen explained, flopping down on the floor and mixing up the parts of the heater.

"I'm beginning to see what you mean," Lila answered, the words heavy on her tongue.

But she hung on, wanting to run after Waldo, yet knowing that she must keep her promise to Allen. For it made sense, didn't it, that Waldo would appreciate not only her love, but her loyalty, her integrity.

The gay life was one thing. But you couldn't build a relationship on temperament alone.

Lila smiled wryly as she put up the water to boil. Danny had been telling her this for years … and now, at last, she was beginning to see what he meant.

And how deeply it could hurt.

CHAPTER EIGHT

ALLEN stayed with her in the Swiss castle until Minnie came down to get him.

"Such a boy," she sighed, shaking her braids. "And you know what, Lila? When he was still high in my belly, I prayed for twins."

Lila listened to Minnie's voice blowing across the vast chasm of her loneliness.

"Look," Minnie said with primitive intuition, "my Isaac is home now. Why don't you come up and say hello? I made a nice *gefüllte* fish. You'll like it."

"Thanks, not now," Lila answered. "I had a late dinner."

"Never too late for a bite," Minnie insisted. "Come, come." She tugged Lila's arm. "Don't be a sucker."

Lila permitted herself to be dragged up the stairs and into the all embracing odor of warm fish spiced with horse radish.

At the table a man with bifocals, low on his long nose, dipped bits of bread into the fish juice and stuffed them into his mouth.

"Sit," Minnie said to Lila as she introduced them.

Isaac looked up. "Here," he said, pushing the bowl of bread toward her. "Eat first. We'll talk later."

Flung the food, Lila had no choice but to mimic Minnie and Isaac, each lost in eating. The fish and sliced carrots, a deep bowl of noodle soup, boiled chicken with mashed potatoes came to her, delivered as the Ten Commandments to Moses.

Lila ate, filling the emptiness of Waldo's absence with the comforting food. After all, she hadn't left forever. A little spat. A moment of temper. Certainly this could not destroy what they felt for each other.

"Now," Isaac said as he pushed back his empty dessert dish.

Lila peered into the gray eyes that smiled at her as he took off his glasses and wiped each lense with a corner of his napkin. He folded the glasses and set them beside his glass of tea and leaned back against the wooden chair. Minnie tilted her head toward him and even Allen was quieter. Isaac, undeniably the head of his household, kept order and sanity supreme.

"I want, first, to thank you for being a good neighbor to my wife," he said. His bushy brown hair puffed out over each ear like a fluffed bird, adding a touch of human softness to the formality of his statement.

Lila started to object.

"And second," he said, overruling her with one raised palm and the lowering of his eyelids, "I want you should know that any friend of Waldo's is a friend of mine."

Startled by this, Lila felt her eyebrows rise.

"I mean it," Isaac continued. "Waldo is a *meshuggeneh,* yes. But I think she is also like me." He paused to sip the pale liquid and remove its soggy slice of lemon. "A refugee. Not from Hitler, perhaps. But from," he pointed one straight finger toward the ceiling, "from God."

Minnie nodded and sighed, as though burdened by the weighty sageness of her husband's pronouncement.

"And you," he proceeded, as though reading a dossier, "are a nice girl. You should run away from Waldo and get married."

Lila tried to suppress a smile. "But you said you were a friend of Waldo's," she murmured.

"That does not stop a man from knowing right from wrong," he said flatly. "Waldo is Waldo. And you are you."

For an instant, Lila resented his intrusion. But then she realized that Isaac spoke out of the balance of fairness in his heart. He was a man who needed no preliminaries, no permission to speak of personal matters. His calm eyes had seen her pain. Why try to deny it? And in his own way, he was trying to help her.

"I am married," Lila said, the truth springing out of her unbidden.

Isaac shook his head. "No. Maybe by law, yes. But in spirit?"

"Leave the girl in peace," Minnie whispered as though Lila couldn't hear her.

"Peace is for hypocrites," Isaac said.

In a far corner of the room, Allen banged his skates together, wanting to be noticed.

"Did you do your homework?" Isaac said without turning in his chair.

Guilty silence answered him.

"My son thinks that the world is like a feast that he can take from it whatever he wants free of charge," Isaac said. "I work in a wig factory to save for my son to go to college. And then he will work and save for his sons to go. That is how the world turns. On work. And on the pleasure of hopes for the next generation. When I say this to Waldo, you know what she does? She laughs at me and lights a cigar."

Minnie sighed again and got up to clear away the dishes with a clatter, telling Isaac thus that he had spoken enough for one night.

"Waldo will be a great painter someday," Lila said with a defensive twist in her voice.

"I hope so," Isaac concluded. "But in the meantime, between the fights, you should feel free to come up here and visit us. I can tell you lots of stories about artists. Real artists, from Budapest," he said with a voice that seemed to yearn for Mecca thousands of miles away.

"Yes," Lila said. "I would like to hear about them."

She got herself to the door and flew down the steps, hoping that Waldo had come back by now.

She flung the door open and stared into darkness. Two and a half hours had passed. Where did Waldo have to go to get a licence?

Lila stalked around the big bare room, telling herself to feel nonchalant. Waldo would come back. Eventually. So why not be casual about it? Why not relax and busy herself with doing something useful instead of giving in to the pinch of anxiety deep in her throat?

But there was nothing to do to keep busy with. No dishes to wash, no furniture to dust. Nothing to dust with, even if there were furniture. Well, she would go downstairs and have a look at the station wagon. No doubt there would be kids sitting on the fenders that she could chase away.

She strode the two blocks, prepared to loose her anger toward Waldo on whomever might be molesting the car.

But there was no one.

Some boys played boxball on the sidewalk. Older ones leaned against a newspaper stand. No one gave a damn about Waldo's car.

Now what?

Lila walked and walked, hoping crazily that she might run into Waldo as she had run into Danny.

Maybe Waldo, in her annoyance, had decided to punish her by purposely staying out late. Maybe she had gone to see Marge.

Lila could picture the two of them, happily taunting Carmen with an intimacy that Carmen could never share.

She found a phone booth and dialed Marge's number, glad now that she hadn't picked up her valise earlier for it would give her such a good excuse.

Hanging on stubbornly, she listened to the buzzes and the pauses. Marge was always home. She had to be home now. She had to be Waldo's harbor so that Lila could always count on finding Waldo there whenever they had a fight.

Nothing.

No Marge.

Not even Carmen with her desperate squeaky voice to say that Waldo had come and gone.

Lila bought herself an Alka Seltzer to spade up the weighty wad of Minnie's cooking, lying like an admonishing judgment in her stomach. The small tapping of a headache was just coming to her attention and she gulped down the fizzy water on a single breath.

Maybe the bars, Lila thought, determined not to give herself up to a passive waiting for Waldo. She had to do something, keep busy, feel like she was making some progress toward the one person in her life who mattered.

And Jingle had shown her the current bars. All of them no doubt, she grimaced to herself. If she followed the track of her subconscious memory, she would find Waldo.

For Waldo, she knew without having to ask, was a night blooming flower. Eventually Waldo, the angry Waldo, would wind up crocked and happy-go-lucky, surrounded by acres of admiring women.

The thought tightened Lila's heart. For what, really, did Waldo yet know of her, to differentiate between her love and that fleeting compliment of another? They had spoken of love, of Waldo's paintings, and of money. She knew Waldo's past, present and future as though they had been living together a thousand years.

But she had told Waldo nothing of herself. Of her own ambitions. Of her fresh emancipation from Danny. She had not told of herself because all this ceased to be important beside Waldo's ambitions. How, then, could Waldo know? She had no raw material for intelligent judgment.

Lila, conceding this to be her own fault, kicked herself down the block, promising the image of Waldo more of herself.

Wind sucked in through her shirt collar and slipped between her breasts to roll coldly around the flat of her stomach and up along her spine. Yet her flesh felt warm beneath the chill. The kindled anticipation of making up with Waldo, of erasing all her defects, drove her on and she felt almost cheerful among the dormant dregs of her misery.

With a strange hope, Lila went first to the coffee house where they had first sat together and felt close. But the faces ignored her or appraised her accessibility.

Bleecker Street and McDougal, like spaded earth, swarmed with live ones turned loose. The garlic odor of pizza hung above parked groups of motor scooters. She pushed through the crowds feeling that at any moment, Waldo's tousled head would pop up among them. Someone pinched her behind and someone else tittered.

"Say, girl, you ought to find yourself a handsome guy."

Lila sailed above it all, her gaze fixed on the distant sun of Waldo's welcoming smile. She nudged into crowded bars, lifted herself onto tiptoes, making the rounds.... Making the rounds.

"Hey, Lila."

Jingle's voice.

She saw his trench coat shoulder through. Turning to run, she felt herself lassoed by his grip.

"Hi, kid," Jingle said, his beard widening in a smile. "Where you going in such a hurry?"

Lila shrugged, not wanting to give away her personal affairs. "Just breezing through."

"Come have a beer," he urged. "Long time no see."

"No thanks," Lila said impatiently. She stared down at his fingers till he released his grip.

"Signed up for school yet?" he said, holding her with his talk.

"Not yet."

"Why not yet?"

"Look, Jingle. I'm in a hurry. Speak to you some other time, all right?"

Jingle put himself in front of her with a casual movement as though he had been moved there by the crowd. "Hurry?" he drawled. "No one hurries in the Village. Don't you know that?"

"I do," Lila said flatly.

Jingle's pointed beard seemed to open her up. "What's the matter, honey? Someone giving you a hard time?"

Jingle knew. She saw it in his too red mouth as it opened over the crossed teeth.

In answer, she made a sudden dive around him but he grabbed her arm again.

"Say, listen, Lila, I didn't mean to louse you up about the apartment."

She heard the serious, apologetic, self-centered concern and felt a knife point of anger cut across her lungs.

"Forget it," she said like thunder.

"I don't like to make enemies," he persisted.

"Then let me pass."

"But, honey. I mean, well, don't give a guy a hard time. I can do things for you, remember?"

"Oh, I remember, all right."

"Tell you what," he said, pressing her cheeks together with his fingertips. "The Cooper exams are coming up next week. I can get 'em for you. Wholesale."

With a sudden thrust of fury, Lila's foot shot out and caught him in one shin. She dove past him and forced through the crowd, steaming in the vapor of her feeling.

It rang through her head what a fool she was. What a mad thing she must look like, bludgeoning around people, her own identity smeared in the blood of her desire to possess Waldo.

She couldn't go down the drain this way. Wash clear out of sight. Become another Village derelict, acting cool and feeling empty.

It was not news to her, this whirlpool round and round into oblivion. She had seen it happen to others. Seen it and felt contempt for it in others.

Now it was happening at home. Lila felt it. She could even predict the stages of its development.

With full knowledge of this, she chased the streets looking for Waldo. Because Waldo was important and Waldo didn't care.

CHAPTER NINE

THE string of bars came to an end.

A dead end.

Eleven-thirty by the clock in a darkened barber shop. There was no place to go now, except back to the loft. To sit and wait, as she dreaded waiting till Waldo would deign to return.

The park rustled its weighty leaves overhead, breathing down a leafy clean odor. A mandolin played in the shadows. Something sprightly with Italian words sparking of the old country, of folk dances, of times gone by ... good times in better days.

Lila, exhausted, flopped down on a bench and stretched out her legs. She felt better about sitting here, until daylight if necessary, than going back to the turpentine and the pictures that spoke of Waldo without revealing her deepest secrets. She lit a cigarette and drew smoke in toward the headache that crackled like lightning behind her eyeballs. A man strolled by, following a skunk tied to a leash.

The Village. Good times, easy living. Doing things that mattered instead of pandering to phony conventions. Lila laughed with an acid twinge. She could tell the world what a fraud, what a hoax it was to be in love in the Village where love was like smoke, sailing high away from its source, anxious to be gone, to disappear.

But the park closed at midnight and the cops would come through to clean the benches of their loiterers. Herself included. Well, she would go home. Work out a budget for Waldo, make program notes of the paintings in case Waldo could use them.

At least this would take up the time.

Time. Kill time. Lila ambled as slowly as her legs would drag, praying without faith that Waldo would be home by now.

She stood across the street from the building and stared up at the black windows. Then she started up the stairs, counting them as she went to keep her mind off the terrible moment of stepping into the dark, alien room.

Lila pushed open the door.

"Hey."

The single word dissolved all horrors, swept out the past hours with their nightmare thoughts.

Waldo sat up on the cot. "Where the hell you been?"

Lila grinned, tilted suddenly into the position of superior advantage. "You could at least put on the lights," she said.

"Forget it. The electric just went off."

"How much is the bill?"

"A hundred and nine dollars. Why?"

"We have to pay it, don't we?"

In the darkness, Waldo came to her. The strong arms brought her in close, bringing back happiness.

"I said, where the hell've you been?" Waldo murmured.

"Out for a stroll," Lila said with cheerful slyness.

She wanted to unburden herself, tell Waldo all about it. But the pain had gone. Mysteriously wiped out. All she knew now was the touch, the vital odor of Waldo's nearness.

"Don't do that again, will you?" Waldo said.

"I might."

Waldo brought Lila down onto her lap, hugging her in close around the waist. "All right," she said. "I'm sorry. But that damned kid. What a time to burst in on us."

"We've got things to finish," Lila murmured, gleeful that desire had been plaguing Waldo all this time. Happy beyond expression that Waldo had been forced to think of her.

"Mmmm," Waldo's cool lips found her throat and moved in slow circles on it.

"Did you get the licence?" Lila pulled slightly away, needing to goad her, to tease her and torment her as she herself had been tormented through the hours.

"Five bucks."

"Do you always have to talk about money?" Lila said.

"But you asked."

"No. I asked if you got the licence, not how much it cost."

"So," Waldo chuckled. "You're devil-may-care about money, are you? What have I got here, a little heiress or something?"

"No. Just somebody who cares about you, not the price of you."

"Like there's a difference."

Waldo's cynicism crackled with brittle judgement.

"Now listen," Lila said, holding herself stiffly on Waldo's thighs. "We're not running a bargain basement here. I'm sick to death of the price tags that go with you. I know what it's been like and that you're tender about money. But climb off the slave market, will you?"

"And trust what fate to keep me floating?"

"Me," Lila said angrily. "And yourself."

"Hah."

"Hah? Why hah?"

"I'm up to my ears with trusting women, baby. Women are all alike, don't you know that? After the first flush of the honeymoon, it's … whammo, get lost, butch."

Lila pulled herself off Waldo's lap and stood glaring down at her in the darkness lessened only slightly by the glare from a street lamp.

"If that's what you think," Lila drilled, "what am I doing here?"

"I dunno, honey. What are you doing here?"

Lila swallowed a rush of tears. This was no time for dreaming, no time for the slop of sentiment.

"Maybe I was kidding myself," she said in a low voice.

"About what?"

"You, Waldo. Maybe you're nothing but a barrel rattling loose coins."

"Maybe."

"Well, answer me, you dope. Don't sit there and feel sorry for yourself. Of course you don't like it. I don't like it much myself, either. But if anything's going to work out between us, you'll have to face up to the practical side of things, just as I'm facing up to it. And you can do it like a man, can't you, for chrissake?"

"Wow, little spitfire," Waldo breathed.

Lila heard the first hint of admiration in Waldo's voice and knew that at last she was coming through to her.

"We'll make out," she said more gently. "If you'll just have some patience and a little faith."

Yet Lila laughed at her own words. She knew that patience and faith were the furthest qualities from Waldo's experience.

"Tell you what," Waldo said. "We'll make a bargain."

She felt Waldo's fingers on her hips, drawing her close.

"What kind of bargain?" Lila said warily, stiffening her knees so that Waldo would not end the night by dissolving her with passion before they got this straightened out.

"I'll promise not to lose my temper, if you promise not to crusade for Utopia around here."

"No go," Lila said bluntly.

Waldo sighed and fished a butt from the ashtray on the floor. "Why not?"

"Because it's not good enough, that's why." Lila took out a fresh pack of cigarettes and handed it to Waldo.

"What do you want, baby? Promises neither of us can keep?"

"Promises we can," Lila dared.

A match flared, lighting the curving rim of Waldo's nostrils. She was breathing hard, pressured by Lila's insistence; forced, Lila knew, to face decisions few women would demand from her.

"When I play," Lila persisted, hoping her heart would stop lolloping so the words might come out straight, "I play for keeps and all the way. You're no little amusement for me, Waldo. I've signed my whole life over to you and I want yours signed back in return."

"Like the car," Waldo breathed.

"Yes, like the car but without the sarcasm."

Lila heard the springs squeak and knew that Waldo had turned away from her to stare at the wall.

"What about it?" Lila pushed. "Can we make a go of it like two human beings or do we call it quits right here and now?"

There was a long silence. The whine of soft tires wheeled through the empty streets.

A hand groped out and caught her own, linking its cold fingers with her damp ones.

"I don't know, Lila," Waldo said, barely audible. "But I'll try for you. I honestly will."

The vise around Lila's heart relaxed. All she wanted, all she needed was Waldo's sincere effort. The rest, she knew she could take care of herself.

She came up close to the cot now and folded herself up beside Waldo, hugging in close to the tense body.

"I believe in us," she whispered. "I really do."

And as Waldo turned to her, the passion she had known earlier transmuted into something tender. It drifted up into Waldo's smiling face, kissed the lips waiting for her, and tiptoed off into a blissful sleep.

CHAPTER TEN

THEY came awake together, moving toward each other through the quiet darkness.

Neither spoke as Lila reached out from her dreamless sleep to touch the outline of ribs breathing evenly against her. They lay pressed together on the cot's narrowness, bodies blending with no room to turn away. She felt surrounded by Waldo's body, engulfed and consumed in it.

Paintings hovered grotesquely above, each silent within the confines of its own being. Yet Lila felt that each held drops of Waldo's blood, of Waldo's life, and that they grinned at her through the darkness, biding their time patiently and unwilling to give up their secrets.

Yet she knew happiness now. Waldo's knee touched her thigh, moving up and down along its curve. She gave herself to Waldo's caresses, spilling the cup of her desire toward Waldo's eager lips. To morrow would be better. Closer, even, than now. Tomorrow they would arise with a new understanding, having seen their first battle to its finish and having conquered it with sense … and with decency.

In decency, Lila lifted her hips, spilling love, sacred as festival wine. And Waldo, tense and trembling, seemed not a refugee from holiness, but a willing penitent.

"Love me," Lila whispered, meaning not by flesh alone.

"I need you," Waldo answered and clasped Lila's hand beneath the blanket.

Waldo's touch grew brutal now, tearing from the forest of their troubles to leap in the spectacle of their mutual joy.

They chased each other onward, goading passion like a plaything, kicking it higher, higher, till it soared among the stars.

Comets flared and Lila shut her eyes before the bursting beauty. Her body, a ritual of loving, twisted in worship at the altar of their ecstasy.

They slept and woke and slept again, newly created with each meeting....

At noontime, they finally climbed out of bed.

Lila stared at her dungarees, heaped on the floor. "I've got to go shopping," she said. "It's a must."

She felt overwhelmed with her need to be perfect for Waldo. To stand on a pedestal for Waldo to admire.

"Well, go then," Waldo laughed. "I have to see about frames for these damned pictures anyway."

"Don't you want to come along?" Lila said, smothering a hint of disappointment.

"Love to, honey. But I can't spare the time. The show opens this week end. There's so much to do."

"Will you have enough cash?" Lila said slyly as Waldo pushed the tails of her dirty shirt into her trousers.

Waldo caught the innuendo and closed one eye. "You conning me?" she said.

"Sort of," Lila admitted. She didn't want to be cheated of certain pleasures. Of seeing Waldo's face when she had bills spread out across her palm.

"I'm supposed to be finished being mercenary," Waldo said around a flattened cigarette.

"Just this one last time," Lila coaxed.

"No. I feel too damned ashamed of myself to take any money from you this day."

She heard Waldo pulling away from her and knew that yesterday had been much too harsh.

Harsh . . but necessary.

"Good," Lila said, being bouncy. "I'd much rather lean on you, you know."

But she saw that Waldo had clicked off her voice. Snapped it right off, like a bad program. Instead she scribbled numbers on a greasy pad with the fat stub of a pencil. Lila peered around her elbow and knew that she was writing frame sizes. The business of the day.

"All right," Lila said in a small voice, anxious not to interfere. "I'll be home by five o'clock. Will you?"

"Mmm hmmm."

Conscious that she couldn't reach Waldo now, Lila finished combing her hair and hurried from the room. She wanted to get out quick, rather than watch Waldo disappear. Better for her hopes. Better for her trust to pretend that last night's break hadn't even happened.

She rushed off to the bank, forcing her mind to juggle balances and withdrawals. Last week, she'd had enough to live on for six months without working. Now, after the expense of Waldo's car and dinners and all the dinners to come, she doubted the possibility of stretching what remained through the summer.

The panic of being broke, of facing Waldo's needs empty handed, pushed her to the telephone. She had been putting off talk of money matters with Danny till the last possible moment. Originally, she had wanted nothing from him but her independence.

But now, her own integrity grew small beside the immediate necessity of providing until such time as Waldo began to make substantial sales.

Danny's hello was calm as only Danny could be calm. Yes, of course they could sit down together and balance the books. Any time she wanted. This afternoon? Good a time as any.

Because Dany would think her slightly mad to arrive in her dungarees, Lila quickly bought a new skirt and blouse. Cheap things, to have money left for Waldo later tonight.

Then she hopped a bus and went back uptown, coming back into the neighborhood of maids and strolling carriages, of doormen whistling for cabs, like a world weary traveller gone these many years.

"Good to see you," Danny said noncommittally as he opened the door to her.

She caught the slight stubble of beard and knew that Danny wasn't as calm as he pretended.

"How are you?" she said like a stranger.

"Fine, Lila, fine. The research is stacking up, of course. But that's to be expected."

His desk, piled with open library books, seemed burdened with his scholarly considerations. Books instead of blood. Thoughts where feelings ought to live. Good sense. Balance. The staid movement of Danny's schedule toward its planned goal.

"There's ginger ale in the fridge," he said but he made no move to get it out.

Lila took down shiny glasses from the cupboard and opened the refrigerator door, knowing that Danny assumed he would be waited on. Her heart clinched tight against all the indignities he had perpetrated on her. The slave of herself that had grown to hate him felt easier now, as she contrasted this with Waldo's love making.

"How's it going?" Danny said, keeping the gaps of their alien thoughts from separating too far.

"Well, thank you."

"Good."

A pigeon on the windowsill made cooing sounds and peered in at them with wide, bare eyes.

"It's almost spring," he said, regarding it.

Once it would have meant that soon they would be going for rides in the country. Picnics near Bear Mountain where they had both loved to breathe the space and the vastness of eons secreted among the trees. Now it meant nothing.

"It was spring four days ago," Lila said like a school teacher marking an examination.

"Oh." Danny set his glass, untouched, on the kitchen table. "Well, down to business," he said, pulling out a chair for her.

"I've got it all worked out," Lila said briskly. "To make it easy for us both."

"Fine. Whatever you say."

"Just this," Lila continued, not looking at him. "If you'll give me the five thousand we were saving toward a house, I'll call it even."

Danny, surprised, let out a low whistle. "That sure is simple," he said. "But it's an awful lot of money, Lila."

"I need it," she said truthfully. "And besides, it would come to that in alimony before you knew it."

"True."

The single word told her that he was digesting her statement, surveying the positive implication of divorce and finding it curious.

"May I ask why the rush?" he said, crossing his legs and observing her as though reading close paragraphs in a text book.

"A girl's got to live," she answered, trying for lightness.

It didn't fool him, she saw. He leaned his weight backward onto two of the chair legs and folded his arms. "What about your own account?" he said clinically.

"That's beside the point." Her brusqueness was the wrong approach to him but she could not stop it. An uneasy feeling that Danny must not find out her true motives made Lila tense.

"I'm sorry," he said slowly. "But it's not beside the point at all. You left me, remember. And with no legal grounds. None, I don't know, Lila, that I owe you more than a certain portion of my salary."

"Don't be a penny pinching squirt," Lila blurted. "Since we can't live together, why make trouble?"

"I don't know that we can't live together," he said with a bull headed stubbornness that goaded her temper.

"Danny, please," she said, choking on her words. "Do you want to kill me? If you want that, just put your hands around my neck and do it fast."

"Save the drama," Danny said evenly. "You know you don't impress me with it."

Lila wished she could turn the table over in his face. Run out and keep going for thousands of miles. But she had responsibilities stronger than her own pride. She must think of Waldo and keep herself under control.

"All right, then," she said, almost choking. "How do you want to settle this?"

"By trying again," he said earnestly. "By acting like people who took their marriage vows seriously."

"Danny, stop it."

"Why?"

Helplessly, Lila's fist pounded the table. "Just stop it," she yelled, swallowing the tears tight in her throat.

Danny waited.

"I'm sorry," she said after a moment. "It's just that you irritate me so."

"You look tired, Lila."

"Never mind that."

Danny lifted his ginger ale and tasted it, squinting in a narrow shaft of sunlight that emphasized the tiredness in his own face.

"What you ought to do," he said, "is go away for a while and think things over. With perspective ... with time ..."

Lila shook her head.

"Don't you owe it to yourself?" he persisted. "Not to me, so much. But to yourself? It's easy enough for two people to get divorced. You can do that any time. Why rush? Why push it when you're in such a state?"

"I've got to be away from you," Lila said.

"I don't believe it," he answered with a firmness that cut her open. "Maybe for a few months, yes. But not permanently. We've had too much together to just let it dry up like that."

"What have we had, Danny?" she said with bitterness. "What exactly have we had?"

Danny's lips pursed with sudden understanding as he listened to the teeter in her voice that spoke of her imbalance, her desperate need for something to hold onto.

"So that's it," Danny said quietly. "You might have told me as much. You know I wouldn't stand in your way, Lila, if I knew he was worth his salt."

Lila wanted to laugh in his face. As though she would ever again give herself to a man. Ever permit it to happen, as it had happened between them.

"There's no man," Lila said, lowering her eyelids to veil the image she saw, felt in the center of her being, of Waldo's touch.

"You don't have to lie, you know. You're a free woman."

Danny's rocklike stupidity bruised. She pushed back the chair and went back to the refrigerator, taking out the half bottle of martini mix that stood beside a small bottle of pearl onions in the cold emptiness.

"If you think," she said deep in her throat, "that I would ever look at another man again ... that I would be so foolish ... so stupid ..." She stumbled, unable to find words low enough for what she felt.

"Then why are you raving?" Danny said, inspecting her with his relentlessness.

"Let's talk about money," she said from between clenched jaws.

"Money comes second. I want to talk about you. Us."

"Forget it."

Danny came up behind her and took away the bottle from her trembling grasp. "How can I?" he said. "You're still my wife. I have memories."

"You're a damned pain in the neck," she said, wanting to wound him, to cut him off before he touched her. "Didn't I see you sitting in the Village the other day like a little lost sheep? Why can't you be a man for once in your life and let me go without smearing all this dirt? Without making me hate you?"

"If you hated me," Danny said, "I'd feel it and let you go. As for being a man … maybe I'm no Rhett Butler, but you used to like it."

"Oh, please, please stop this," she pleaded with desperation. "Can't you see?"

He looked at her in silence for a long time. Then his hands fell away from her shoulders and he took in a deep breath.

"Yes, I think I see, Lila," he said slowly. "But whoever you're going to spend our money on, just remember what's for sale and what isn't."

She heard the acquiescence in his tone and instantly discarded all the rest. What could he know about her hopes, her love for Waldo? What had he ever known beyond his own selfish ambitions, his own greed?

Lila kept her silence, her mind already rushing ahead to Waldo, as Danny made arrangements for the transfer of their savings to her own name.

CHAPTER ELEVEN

"THE first thing we need," Lila said, kicking parts of the heater to the wall, "is a decent apartment."

"What's wrong with this one?"

"Everything," Lila laughed. "How can I keep house for you without a kitchen? Besides, I don't care for johns in the hall."

"You're spoiled."

"I want to spoil you."

Waldo's smirk told Lila she had said the right thing but at the wrong time.

"Spoil me, honey. But do it after the summer. Marge'll be over to help with these picture frames. Who's got time to hunt down apartments?"

"You didn't tell me about Marge," Lila said quickly.

Waldo shrugged. "So I'm telling you now."

"And when we get the apartment," Lila persisted, "we need new friends. Nice, stable people who'll be a good influence on you."

"The only influence I need is a write-up in the Sunday *Times*. That kind of people you can always bring around."

Lila felt she was rapidly getting nowhere. She had five thousand dollars to shine her world bright, but somehow, this hadn't impressed Waldo as she'd expected. The woman seemed made out of mist. She could reach out to Waldo and her fingers would go right on through, grasping nothingness.

"What time will Marge be here?" Lila said glumly.

"Soon as she rounds up Whitey."

"Who the hell is Whitey?" Lila blurted, letting a canvass slip to fall on her foot.

"One of her influences," Waldo answered blandly. "You better like her."

Then Lila remembered hearing the name and leafed through her collection to place Whitey in the Provincetown gallery. She fell silent. How could she argue about someone who was good for Waldo's career?

"I'll like her," she said obstinately, "if I choke."

"Don't worry, honey, you won't."

Lila heard a curious fuzz over Waldo's tone that slapped her like cold water. She wanted suddenly to ask a million questions about this Whitey. How long Waldo had known her. If they had ever slept together. Why, if she was so damned influential, she hadn't helped Waldo already.

But the words stuck in her throat. Lila knew that if they came out, she would sound like a nagging *hausfrau*. And besides, in a few minutes she would have Whitey there in the flesh.

Waldo, who had brought back sandwiches along with the frames, unwrapped waxed paper and crumpled it, tossing the ball onto a pile of them beneath the window.

"Tell you what," Waldo said quietly, "go on upstairs and take one of Minnie's nice, hot showers."

"I don't need to be fussed over," Lila said, sorting out lengths of wood. Waldo hadn't even asked what she had been doing all afternoon. She felt, strangely, that if she dropped dead in the middle of Forty-Second Street, Waldo would be the last one to find out.

Waldo swallowed down hunks of dry sandwich. "I didn't mean to humor you," she mumbled. "I only thought you'd want to look your best ..."

"For you?" Lila snapped. "Or for Whitey?"

She saw Waldo's lips go white and knew she had hit the black center of some vulnerability. "I'm sorry," she added quickly.

"Everything seems to be going wrong today. I don't know why. It just is."

Waldo grunted, which added to Lila's sense of lost control. With everything in disorder, the apartment, their future, Lila's need for neatness ached with a vague throbbing. She felt it spreading throughout her, like an infection threatening to eat away the parts that were still good.

"I'll take you up on that shower," she said now, needing to be alone, to collect the scattered remnants of herself.

She set the wood down carefully and grabbed the dirty towel.

Climbing to Minnie's place was like lifting herself out of a dank basement into some country garden.

Minnie, weilding a potholder, said, "So *nu?* Is the *meshuggeneh* hammering her head off or just the fingertips?"

Despite herself, Lila had to smile. "It's all for the sake of art," she said, knowing that Minnie could never understand.

"I saw those paintings," Minnie stirred noodles, holding her face away from a blossom of steam.

The judgment came across to Lila in the finesse of silence. But she was in no mood to defend Waldo. If anything, she needed a little defense herself and wished that Minnie had the power to go downstairs and shake Waldo rightside up.

"I brought my own soap," Lila said, clutching a blackened sliver.

"Go already," Minnie said. "Before my Allen comes home from the movies and nabs you."

"I like Allen," Lila said truthfully. "He has imagination."

"A little less imagination we could all do without."

Lila proceeded to the metal shower of Isaac's handiwork and stripped naked. Her breasts felt sore and puffy, her belly too bloated from eating odd foods at disagreeable hours. She had been a creature of routine and Waldo's way of living was a hardship she could not deny. Her armpits itched and the backs of her feet felt scaly. She was coming apart at the seams and each cell of her flesh objected to the revolution.

She turned on the hot water. It trickled at first, then spurted full, making a tinny thunder against the hollow sides of the cubicle. Stretching her neck far backward, she let the hot stream pulse against her throat and burn down along her chest to dribble away along the tense muscles of her thighs. Enveloped in a thick lather, she felt for the moment safe and warm. If only she could wrap up inside a large turkish towel and go to sleep with Waldo beside her. If only there was no one new to meet, no one to be sweet to. If only the five thousand dollars, wrenched from Danny... and unfairly... could be spread like a canopy over Waldo's head to block out all views of a treacherous world. If... if...

Lila soaked in the scalding stream, letting the anger drain away into a lethargic peace.

Maybe Waldo would make good sales at the Village show. Maybe she would find success, suddenly, like the Holy Grail. Maybe all the turmoil would come rapidly undone and spread a magic carpet for them to fly away on.

Maybe... if... maybe...

Lila laughed at her pipe dreams. You could count on nothing with Waldo, except the moment. You lace up your fears and jump into the fray like a good football player. You be tough. You smile.

Always, you smile.

Lila rubbed herself dry and mopped up the spots of water that had flown free of the shower stall. She put on the new skirt again and zippered it over the fresh blouse, remembering that Waldo had not even bothered to comment on them.

But Lila suspended judgement, sensing that in the strong light of criticism, Waldo might come apart like a fragile insect.

When Lila came out of the bathroom, she left her thoughts behind, stepping forth into the arena where she must do battle and prove herself strong, her love stronger than the various lights that shimmered on and off in Waldo's world.

After all, there were no wrinkles in her new clothes yet. And she might even impress Whitey. Wouldn't Waldo be surprised at that?

Thinking of Whitey prepared Lila for their meeting so that her jaw did not drop when she stepped into the room.

"How do you do," Whitey said, wielding a polished black cane and lifting an arched white eyebrow above her glinting monocle. As she lifted the cane, bracelets dropped to her wrists, golden serpents that clattered.

Lila wished she had something to lean against as she smiled tentatively at the grandiose figure of a woman, fifty years, if she were a day, dominating the loft, subduing not only Marge and Carmen, but Waldo too, who strode nervously about with thumbs hooked tight into her belt loops.

"How do you do," Lila answered properly to the long face beneath its masses of iron gray hair.

She had seen straight posture in her life, but this tall woman, full bosomed beneath a dress of black crepe that gave off perfume like incense, appeared suspended by a plumb line.

It was too comical, Lila thought, easing herself down onto the cot. The dowager matron idolized by a gathering of little sea shell butches. Instantly, Lila knew that Waldo had tried to make her and had failed. That Marge, too, had tried and failed. The temptation of the unavailable, substituting mystery for sex appeal.

And Waldo, completely hypnotized, was at a loss for words, sputtering around the room like a panting little engine straining uphill.

Marge, busy with a miter and fitting frames, camouflaged her own edginess.

"Of course you like them," Waldo bombasted as Augustine White pointed her cane first at one, then another of the canvasses. "They're great. Haven't I been telling you that for years?"

Lila, subdued in her own corner, sensed that Whitey wasn't so impressed as Waldo might wish.

"Not yet great, my dear," Whitey said, her words well enunciated. "But with application, perhaps with a trifle more feeling…"

"Feeling? What the hell do you call this?" She kicked one huge canvas. "Soft boiled eggs?"

Whitey turned to Lila. "And with whom do you agree?"

"I don't know that much about painting," Lila said simply.

She felt Whitey smiling at her as the monocle came to rest against the cleavage of her ample chest. "That, at least, is honesty," she said.

Carmen looked up from the hammers and nails to grin quickly at Lila. Then, before Marge caught her, she pulled her face down again to the work.

"Look," Waldo said, rocking back onto her heels, "did you come here to choose or complain? All I asked you for was space in your show this summer. If you want to give it to me, fine. If not, let's call it quits right now."

Lila wished Waldo would shut up.

"Patience," Whitey said, unperturbed. "I choose with my eyes, you know. Not with my ears."

This took Waldo down a notch and she quieted with a small, complaining grunt.

The room fell into silence, except for the ever-present hammering. Lila, with her hands folded on her lap, could see that Waldo had much to learn from a person like Whitey if she could only forget her ego and attend to business. She felt thankful that Whitey was wise enough to ignore Waldo's flauntings. Wise and patient and interested in the art divested of its negative perpetrator.

"Yes, I'll take these," Whitey said at last. "When will you bring them up?"

"Monday," Waldo said curtly.

"Good," Whitey answered with genuine pleasure. "And bring your friend," she added without looking at Lila. "The dunes are beautiful on the Cape this time of year."

Lila felt three faces shoot sharp glances at her, as though to say: *what the hell have you got?*

But she could only shrug innocently and stare back at them, the triumph of it dubious, certainly hollow, since she could do no more for Waldo than Waldo had already done for herself.

When Whitey had gone and was safely out of hearing, Marge said, "You've got it made, kid," and smirked at Waldo in the lengthening shadows.

"Crap," Waldo said bluntly.

"Well, why not?" Marge said with an amused civility. "If Whitey likes her ..."

"I said crap," Waldo repeated. "Lila's got to stay here and mind the display. Whether Whitey wants it that way or not, I'm going up alone."

"You dope," Marge said with a nail between her teeth.

Lila came up from the cot. "Now, you two just hold on."

"I said she's staying here," Waldo continued to Marge, ignoring Lila's interruption. "No one's ever gonna say I made my name by ass peddling and that's the truth."

"Who says peddle?" Marge persisted. "You know Whitey has a weakness for young, sweet things. So what if Lila softens her up a little? Nobody can paint your pictures for you, no matter what the size of your stable, hear me?"

"I said shut up!" Lila shrieked. "Both of you."

"Whoops," Waldo said.

"What do you think I am, anyway?" Lila continued, trembling. "I'll damned well make up my own mind about whether I go or stay here and don't either of you forget it."

Waldo patted her quivering shoulder. "Sure, honey, don't mind us."

"But I do mind. I mind very much. It's like I'm not alive, the way you're batting me back and forth."

"Don't take it seriously," Marge said. "You know, the first flush of excitement. Whitey has a way of doing that to people. Building up their hopes. She can make Waldo the talk of the town overnight. You'll just have to pardon our enthusiasm over the very rare fact that Whitey took a liking for you."

"Well, I'm not impressed," Lila answered in a somewhat quieter voice.

"But you ought to be," Marge insisted.

"Leave her alone," Waldo put in. "Lila's got values that you never dreamed of, haven't you, honey?"

"It's a good thing for you," Lila answered, staring straight up into Waldo's smiling eyes. "Or you'd be hanging out of some garbage can with arms and legs dangling."

"I know, I know," Waldo purred. "But you do want to stay in New York, don't you?" She kissed Lila's cheek with an intimate affection.

"Maybe," Lila said, feeling rotten in her stomach at the memory of Waldo carrying on like a eunuch rooster. "But I'll have to think about it."

She turned her back on them all, lighting a cigarette and puffing at it furiously, trying to smoke away the image of her Waldo behaving like a fool. It was one thing to act like a temperamental artist in front of the girls. Quite another to kick around as she had before the eyes of a woman like Whitey.

Lila turned a little to survey the painting that Carmen balanced between her legs. She stared at the blues and the greens and the yellows, measuring them with a cold fierceness. It occurred to Lila for the first time that maybe these pictures really weren't as great as she had assumed, after all.

But the thought slipped away from her, like a body throwing off poison. Her head felt woozy with all that had happened, with the blatant challenge of Whitey's offered friendship.

Maybe she could work a barter somehow.

Maybe, if Whitey really liked her, Waldo could come to see through the eyes of this woman she so highly respected.

Thoughts of manipulation, internal writhings for Waldo's love, turned sour and cynical on Lila's tongue.

"Come on," she said glumly. "Let's quit for a while and go get something to drink."

CHAPTER TWELVE

MIRACULOUSLY, the hours passed, gliding away in a haze. At four, they closed the bars. Carmen and Marge stumbled into a cab to head for home.

Alone with Waldo at last, Lila thought it best to walk for a few blocks, air all the smoke from her lungs, work off some of the liquor that made her footsteps uncertain. She felt like she was walking inside a slowly turning barrel, striding forward but getting nowhere.

Then they were home again and Waldo, not needing sleep, set herself by candlelight to the remaining pictures that needed to be framed.

"You go to bed," Waldo said abstractedly. "We've got a big day tomorrow."

Big day. Lila wanted to laugh in her face. The days seemed all the same to her. Fighting, making up. Feeling alien. Hoping for better luck, for the sudden success that would end their troubles.

As Lila drifted into dreams, she thought of Whitey and her no-nonsense attitude toward Waldo. Whitey, like a breath of truth in the midst of all this sham.

She awoke squinting into a ribbon of bright sunlight. Shuffling footsteps, the noise of pictures being carted to the door jostled her vagrant thoughts.

Lila rolled herself tight into the blankets and watched Jingle's arms stretching to stack the canvases neatly.

"Hi, early bird," he said and winked.

His expression told Lila that their last meeting had been forgotten. She sighed and wiggled her toes, entwining them in the sheets. A good thing that Jingle had such a convenient attitude toward people. He would be perfect for public relations, she thought.

"Where's Waldo?" Lila yawned. She could hardly kid herself that Jingle didn't know the score by now.

"Getting things into the car," he said. "Coming?"

"Where to?"

"To help set things up. Where else?"

Jingle was being sweet. Telling her she was needed. Making her part of the hectic goings on. But she couldn't help wondering if Waldo actually needed her or if she would only be in the way.

"In a sec," Lila said, choosing to be optimistic.

She bounded from the cot and pulled on the old dungarees.

"Take those two small ones," Jingle directed as he started down the steps with the larger canvasses balanced under either arm.

Lila ran a comb quickly through her short hair and dotted on a bit of lipstick, wanting to look fresh and bright for Waldo though she didn't expect Waldo to notice her until later on when all arrangements had been completed.

Then she carried her assigned pictures down to the street and spotted the wagon double parked across the street. Waldo, leaning in over the tail gate, took canvasses from Jingle.

"Good morning," Lila said airily as she handed over hers.

"Well, look who's here," Waldo grinned. "How do you feel?"

"How do you feel?" Lila retorted, eying the gauze of lines around Waldo's lashes.

"Great," she boomed, crawling inside on her knees to batten canvasses properly. "We're in luck with this weather, aren't we, kid? The Village'll be crowded this weekend like nothing you ever saw."

Waldo felt full of herself, like a gas balloon riding high. Lila saw this and felt thankful. Today, at least, would go smoothly. She let herself open to Waldo's excitement.

"Stay here while I go give Jingle a hand," Waldo said, buzzing Lila on the cheek as she passed.

Lila leaned against the rear fender and watched Waldo sprint between two trucks and disappear through the doorway. She watched to catch a glimpse of Waldo's face in the window, then saw Allen's in the window above, waving his cowboy hat at her. Lila waved back, hoping with a tight ache that soon she would be able to go up and tell Minnie that Waldo, Waldo the *meshuggeneh,* had sold paintings and was on her way to fame and glory.

In the sun, in the spring air, she could give herself to this daydream. Believe it true. Lean toward it, feel herself sway around the turning point to success.

Waldo and Jingle came down together carrying the last of the pictures.

"Get inside," Waldo said.

Obediently, Lila climbed into the front seat and watched through the rear view mirror as Waldo locked the back gate with Jingle inside.

"We're off," Waldo said, sliding in beside her and starting up the engine.

Lila asked no questions. She would go where she was taken.

The Buick crept and lurched through the slow moving traffic, coming finally to park on Fifth Avenue some blocks north of the great arch that carved grandeur into the sky.

"It's a great spot, don't you think?" Jingle said conversationally to Lila as he jumped out and began unloading the pictures.

"Here's your seat," Waldo said, folding open a director's chair. "And sandwiches." She emptied her pockets of two bulky ones, piling them on the chair arm. "And coffee." Carefully she set the thermos on the sidewalk.

Lila grinned.

"Think I'd forget you?" Waldo whispered as she passed by Lila on her way to help Jingle.

Lila set herself into the chair and permitted the warmth of her feeling to rise again toward Waldo. The off-handed touches of consideration mixed in with Waldo's self-preoccupation convinced Lila, as no kisses could convince her, that she was loved. Truly. Sincerely. Why, then, fight with the quirks of Waldo's personality? Why try to change her? Why insist that Waldo live, as she obviously could not, like a middle class man?

No. Their love was different. It had to be. Different from convention. And stronger, too. If no legal bonds held them together, certainly their mutual understanding must.

Lila relaxed, watching the pictures going up against the building to display, to reveal the tender core of Waldo's being to the world.

Along the building and across the street, other pictures were going up. Other chairs. A beach umbrella. The competition, in gold frames and no frames. Other efforts, carefully worked out during the winter, disciplined into tangible results of color and composition.

Lila cradled the sandwiches on her lap, feeling a lovely surge of confidence that Waldo's paintings would outdo them all.

"That's fine," Waldo said at last, standing back with hands on hips, perspiration glinting on her neck and her breathing shallow. "Just move that one to the left side and we've got it made."

She sounded all confidence. Not brash as she had to Whitey. But calm and businesslike.

Waldo looked down at Lila. "Well, what do you think?"

"I liked it better on the right," Lila said.

"Move it back again," Waldo called. "The lady here has the last word."

Jingle moved it back.

"Okay?" he said, peering at them both through the sun.

"Good," Lila said, enjoying her moment of authority.

"Okay," Waldo echoed.

Lila unscrewed the thermos cap. "You two have a slug," she said, feeling happily abundant.

"I need a beer." Jingle wiped his face. "How about you?"

"Not just now," Waldo said to him. "I have a confab to finish," she nodded toward Lila.

"Then I'll be running along."

"Thanks, Jingle. You'll drop by the place tonight?"

Jingle glanced at Lila. He seemed to be chewing something inside his small mouth and the point of his beard bobbed. "If I can make it," he said slowly.

Waldo squatted beside Lila as Jingle strolled away. She clasped her dirtied hands together and pressed forearms to either knee, balancing easily.

"Well?" Waldo said in a small voice.

"It's beautiful," Lila said, trying to pump up enthusiasm. "We're going to do just fine, darling. I don't want you to worry about it for a second."

Waldo nodded with a sigh. A lock of hair curled over her ear. "This is my third year, you know," she said with a release of private dubiousness.

"But it's different now," Lila said, touching the sweatshirt caked with dirt.

"Different? How?"

"You've got me," Lila said softly. "I'm your good luck penny." She had meant to be cute, to be feminine, to soothe Waldo with magic assurance.

Waldo raised an eyebrow. "I'll take your word for it. But don't let the bums get you down."

"The who?"

"Oh, you'll see for yourself. The kibitzers. The smart guys. You're too damned beautiful to sit here all by yourself and expect to draw only the lovers of art."

"Don't worry. I can handle them."

"Think so?"

"Of course," Lila laughed. "I may have been born yesterday. But, honey, you made me grow up mighty fast."

She saw Waldo release a little smile. "I know I give you a hard time," she said softly. "But if you can't take me, who can?"

Lila suppressed an urge to lean over and kiss her. "I said you're not to worry, hear me?"

"That's a deal," Waldo answered, standing up to stretch the stiffness from her knees. She pulled a bit of paper from a back pocket and pressed it into Lila's hand. "If you catch a fish," she said, "those are the prices."

Lila glanced at the numbers and felt a little chill rise along the inside of one arm. "Expensive, aren't we?" she breathed.

"We're not selling doughnuts."

Lila heard Waldo's annoyance and cut off the argument about to launch from her on matters of good sense and money.

"I see you never worked in a store, though," Lila said mildly.

"Damned right. My father was a lobsterman in Maine and money didn't come rolling in on the waves, I can tell you. But I'm going to make up for it, every bit."

It was the first Lila had heard about Waldo's past and she wished they were alone someplace where she could hear the whole story.

"Well, we owned a dry goods store in Poughkeepsie," Lila traded. "And money didn't come rolling in by the bolt either." She smiled. "So that makes us about even."

Morning ripened around them as they chatted. Couples strolled by, paused to watch the preparations being completed, to criticize among themselves or trade aesthetic talk. Talk that came cheap without the price of work behind it to soften brisk evaluations of talent, of suitability, of finished work.

"Yep, the horses are at the lineup," Waldo said, following Lila's gaze.

"Let's see where they finish," Lila added, persistently cheerful.

In silence now, they observed the comings and the goings. Lila felt strangely naked to be part of this, eyed by the strollers, evaluated as though it were her work, her soul being offered for sale. She caught her first glimpse of why Waldo had been so callous and so tender at the same time. There seemed to her something horrible about this exposure of self in a frame. And she realized now that the prices Waldo had set down were not too high, but merely an evaluation of her own ideals.

"Look," Lila said, touching Waldo's fingertips with her own. "You must be tired. Why don't you run along home and catch a nap? I'll mind the store and you can check by later."

She saw Waldo's grateful, trusting, open smile.

"All right, honey. I could use it."

With peace in her heart, Lila watched Waldo amble down the streets toward home.

CHAPTER THIRTEEN

IT took only an hour for Lila to feel like a wild animal in a cage. The single men who passed glanced for a moment at the paintings, then tried to look down her blouse as though it were her body that was for sale. Sun glared up from the pavement. She finished the coffee that sickened her with its sweetness. Her throat yearned for something cool, her tongue for the touch of ice.

"Say, what's this supposed to be? A zebra on a stick?"

Lila tried not to hear the comment. Aloofly, she turned her chin away.

"Can't you see what it is, silly? A fried egg. Just get all that yellow."

Couples, arms entwined, clean shaven men with their groomed women, chattered intimately, unafraid, oblivious to Lila's feelings. She could imagine what Waldo must have gone through during the last seasons. Waldo, with her pride raging through, needing to hit out, to fight back at all the cruelty so casually inflicted.

"Maybe you've got a nice nude?" said a voice over her shoulder. "Something about twelve by twenty seven?"

She turned to the big bellied man licking his lips.

"Try down the block," Lila said coldly, wishing she could steer him right into the ocean.

"I'm a divorced man," he continued, ignoring her brush off. "Is this an unfriendly town or what?"

"I wouldn't know."

"Didn't you paint them things?"

"No."

"Then who did?"

"An artist," Lila spat. "A real artist. Now, why don't you run along home?"

"All I want is a nude. Something with …" He grabbed either side of his flabby chest and shook it.

"Get moving, buster."

Lila could feel a shell hardening over her face, over her heart. All she could do was watch the sun go slowly down behind the arch and wonder when Waldo would come back. Pull things in for the night. Release her from this duty so that they might forget all the harshness and plan for tomorrow.

She stood up and walked in a small circle around the chair. Some feet away, a young boy read the Chess Review, managing calmly to ignore all the people. Another hardened character, Lila thought. She wondered why, if he didn't expect to sell, he bothered with this in the first place.

"Would you like this sandwich?" she called to him, needing company.

He looked up and blinked at her through heavy, black framed glasses.

"You got it to spare?" he said with a touch of eagerness.

"Take it." She brought the sandwich to him and put it into his thin, green spattered fingers. "Why don't I watch for both of us," she offered, "and you run up the street for some soda?"

"Great."

She dumped change from her pocket into his free hand and watched him trot away, his khaki pants too large and drooping behind. Turning then to his pictures, she saw clown faces, all sad, all the same. As though he were caught in a rut of wistfulness.

When he came back with the bottles, Lila sucked at hers gratefully, feeling the cold liquid wash down, dissolving grit from the buses exploding exhaust fumes as they passed.

"Two weeks of this," he said, shaking his head. "You better bring yourself something to read," he advised, "or you'll go balmy."

"That's for sure," Lila agreed.

She returned to her chair and sank back against its wobbly material, contemplating the zebra on a stick and seeing it thus, despite herself. A wave of disloyalty swept through her and she forced the image from her mind. For these pictures were all she had of Waldo at the moment. She must be as true to them as she was to the woman herself. Yet she couldn't help wondering what Whitey really thought of the ones she had chosen for her gallery.

The sound of a familiar motor shut off behind her and Lila turned, a smile already blooming on her lips.

It faded quickly as she saw not Waldo, but Marge at the wheel. No Waldo anyplace.

Nerve, Lila thought. Nerve, letting her drive our brand new car.

Still, she couldn't let this show. And along with her annoyance, she knew the knife edge of her own pettiness for such a possessive thought over just a hunk of tin.

"Hi," Marge said, leaning from the open window. "How's it going?"

"The way you'd expect," Lila answered dourly.

"No doubt."

Lila waited but Marge made no motion to get out of the car or to offer relief from her tour of duty.

"Where's Waldo?" Lila asked logically.

"Packing," Marge answered idly.

She didn't like the look in Marge's eyes. The withdrawal, as though the question were out of bounds.

"Packing? What's she got to pack?" Lila continued, feeling ashamed to be asking questions of Marge, who was supposed to be an outsider.

"Her clothes. What'd you expect?"

"Waldo has no clothes," Lila said definitely.

Marge shook her head in patient answer to Lila's naïveté. "She keeps her things at my place where they'll be safe from the paint."

"Oh."

"Waldo asked me to come by for the pictures when it gets dark," Marge said off-handedly.

"You mean she's not coming herself?" Lila blurted, knowing she had nothing whatever to hide from Marge.

"Saves time this way."

"Well, it's not dark yet," Lila said stubbornly, wanting none of Marge's fingerprints on the precious paintings in her care.

"I thought you'd appreciate getting through an hour earlier," Marge shrugged.

"Thanks, but I'll wait."

"Suit yourself, honey. I'll be round again in an hour."

Lila wanted to yell at Marge not to call her honey. Honey. The word of supposed endearment meant nothing, coming from Marge. Empty syllables to substitute for feeling. She hardly could believe that just the other day, she and Marge had been... And now Carmen... Musical chairs.

Lila put her face in her hands to clear away the horrible taste of it all.

She heard the Buick turn a corner, its transmission whining a little in Marge's careless touch. This present that she had given to Waldo, this offering of faith, this commitment of self, what was it to Waldo but just another car?

The boy, who had been listening, said, "I guess I'll be packing up, too," as though telling her it was all right to give in an hour earlier.

She watched him gather his pictures and lug them on a dolly around the corner and into a battered panel truck. It seemed to her more appropriate, this truck, not snappy, not show-off like the Buick. If only she could find that something in Waldo that was down to earth. The sensible thread woven into her bravado.

Gaps, like punched out teeth, began to appear in the lineup of paintings along the street and Lila guessed that it really was all right to close down now.

But she couldn't do anything till Marge got back. And that would be a while, she realized, for she had angered Marge. Marge the poetess. Marge the delicate artist with sensitive nerve ends.

Lila felt sick to death of artists, wearied from their self-centered preoccupations, bored with the ornateness of their flamboyance.

And Waldo... Waldo in the very center of it all. Packing. Packing to go where?

To Whitey, of course.

Probably looking forward to a comfortable room, walks along the water, the continuance of her hopeless flirtation with a woman who really disdained her.

But Waldo was too stupid to know that Whitey disdained her. Or too blind. Always, that persistence of ego. Like a veteran of foreign wars limping bravely to the rhythm of her personal brass band.

Slowly, Lila gathered the canvasses in preparation for Marge's return. Something steely inside her turned slowly to hate. Yes, she hated all the stupidity and all the bombast. Hated the dramatic tumult that surrounded this business of art. Hated the innocent stubbornness that could make such a fool of Waldo.

Hated her. And loved her, too. Because Waldo, in being human, in being vulnerable, made Lila know—as she had never known with Danny—how much she was needed.

CHAPTER FOURTEEN

THE sun had been down half an hour before Marge returned.

"Now are you ready?" Marge called.

Lila felt like a child being punished. Silently, she carted canvasses.

"I ought to tell you," Marge said when Lila got in beside her, "that you aren't being exactly smart."

"I don't have to be smart," Lila said, not knowing exactly what Marge was getting at.

"People who aren't smart," Marge said, "wind up at the bottom of the heap."

Lila smelled the touch of liquor on Marge's breath and knew that she would be favored with volubility beyond Marge's usual secretive way.

"We used to be good friends," Marge said. "Why shouldn't I tell you?"

Lila saw that the car was heading back to the loft. She could only hope that Waldo was home by now.

"Tell me what?" Lila said to pass the time as gently as possible until she could run from this person who used others for her own benefit.

"That you're doing it all wrong."

"I do things my way," Lila responded, fiddling with the radio. "That's good enough for me."

"Is it?"

"It better be." Lila snapped off the music, knowing she was in no mood for irritations. "You stick to Carmen and I'll stick to Waldo, is that a deal?"

For answer, Marge laughed with a loud guffaw. "Cling to Waldo, you mean, like a baby to mommy's breast."

"Let Waldo be the judge of that. And it's none of your business anyway."

"Just being friendly."

"You're friends like a boa constrictor, Marge. I never saw you quite clearly until just this week. But I'm not condemning. All I want you to know is that I'm going to have a private life with Waldo whether you object or the President objects. I know what a fool I must look like to all of you. So what?"

"I better shut up," Marge said thickly. "Forgot to whom I was talking, little Miss Priss."

She drove the rest of the way in silence, her mouth clamped tight, eyes fixed on the road.

Lila lit the last of her second pack of cigarettes, needing something to do with her hands. Marge was talking like this, she knew, because something had begun to irritate her. Maybe Carmen was running out of money, or wising up and getting ready to move out. She couldn't tell exactly what thorns Marge was sitting on, but a restless Marge was a Marge who needed to pass the time.

"One thing I promise you," Lila said, breaking the silence. "If you try to come between Waldo and me, I'll fix you good."

It wasn't a threat, she felt. There was nothing grand in her manner as she spoke the words. Merely a statement of intention.

"Now, now," Marge said. "Don't get in a huff."

Lila listened for signs of guilt and heard only satisfaction. It thrilled her with something like dread.

"All fall out," Marge said as they reached Waldo's building. "We can leave the pictures in the car overnight."

Lila glanced quickly up to the window and saw that it was dark. She remembered the unpaid light bill and kicked herself mentally.

Waldo might be upstairs. She might be elsewhere. Impossible to tell.

"Has she finished her packing?" Lila said acidly.

"Don't worry, honey." Marge leaned over the steering wheel and smiled something benign and evil. "Your bunny rabbit'll be home to you tonight."

"That isn't what I asked."

"Aren't you the darndest. Why don't you hire a detective if you're so damned insecure?"

So Marge was stalling her.

Lila took a breath.

Would Waldo feel annoyed if she came around to get her? Was that acting like a clinging vine?

Better, perhaps, to play it cool and go on upstairs, to wait again in the dark, as though Waldo's comings and goings didn't matter?

Could Waldo, that part of Waldo that was so tender, really be satisfied by a woman who played it cool?

"I'm coming with you," Lila said suddenly, counting on her memory of Waldo's passion to steer her right.

"Oh, my," Marge said with razor edged lips. "What a drag."

Lila hopped into the seat. "I'll take my chances on that," she said, wavering between faith and fright.

As they drove westward, Lila tried on various attitudes of complacency, nonchalance, stubborn assurance and settled, temporarily, for a very distant withdrawal from Marge.

The old contempt she had known during her married life with Danny returned now fully matured to take Marge's brush off with a grain of salt. "If she's so smart, why ain't she rich," as Danny always said.

No, Marge wasn't to be hated, but pitied. Marge, who couldn't sell her poetry or give away her heart. Marge, who could not love but only take, as though greed and selfishness were the highest good. She could see that Marge was on an elevator ride descending steadily downward. In ten years from now, what would she have? Gray hairs and more cynicism. Not to be envied. Certainly not to be emulated.

"I'll tell you something that's going to make you laugh," Lila said quietly, remembering what Isaac had said of Waldo.

"I could use a laugh," Marge said, honking at a diaper van in front of them.

"What you need," Lila said, "is *faith*."

"Oh, wow."

And Marge laughed as Lila had known she would, raucously and with a kind of queasy self-assurance.

Yet it served Lila's purpose, for it gave Marge warning of her own unshakable faith. Faith in what she could not exactly define. Maybe in Waldo. Maybe in the combination of herself and Waldo battling this thing through to a happy finish. Or maybe in *fate*. For Marge's meddling could never shake whatever *destiny* had in mind for all of them.

"Tell me more," Marge said at last. "You make me feel young again."

But Lila felt surfeited. She knew she would not say another word till she spoke with Waldo.

Lila left Marge to park the long car where she could and ran past the lineup of garbage cans in the hallway, flying up the six flights with the energy of her expectation.

"Waldo."

Her voice rang through the small apartment and bounced off random pots and pans.

"Waldo?" she repeated more quietly, peering around corners as though Waldo were a little mouse hiding, perhaps, under a chair.

The door opened and she expected Marge to come in and mock her with the last laugh.

"Hello," Carmen said, taking off a pink coat that flared too long around her thick legs. "Where's Marge?"

"Parking the car," Lila said tiredly, wanting to put her arms around Carmen's neck and weep. "Did you have a hard day?"

"No worse than usual," Carmen said, trying for the contentment of oblivion. "Whose car?"

"Waldo's."

She hung up her coat and began braiding the greasy lank of her hair. "I'd better start fixing supper," she said. "Marge gets into awful fits when she's hungry."

The door boomed wide and Marge burst in on them. Her glance flicked around the room and Lila knew that she, too, was seeking for Waldo. A small flare of triumph stirred deep within her.

"I'm getting supper right away," Carmen said breathlessly.

"You can't know," Marge said, staring at the round, cowering body, "how unglad I am to see you."

Lila fled. She could not bear to witness this thing that Marge must do. Nor could she in any way help Carmen to see the futility of her devotion. She must tend to her own garden.

And that meant finding Waldo.

Lila hopped into a taxi and prayed, all the way home, that tonight shouldn't turn into another of the circumnavigations. She could take no more of the pelting anxiety, the draining of nerves into alcohol. No, tonight she must have surcease. Her thighs began to tremble with a sudden craving for Waldo's nearness. Her lips tingled with kisses to give and to share.

She flung the driver a bill and raced up the stairs, knowing that if Waldo were not there, she would burst.

"Hey, where you been?" Waldo yelped as she flew through the doorway.

"Oh, baby!"

With no words of explanation, Lila yielded herself to Waldo's embrace, shutting her eyes against sense, against the need for talking.

"Just hold me," she whispered, aware of a new fragrance emanating from Waldo. The smell of soap. Clean and good. To her cheek came the crackle of a freshly starched shirt. Her hands slipped down to touch new gabardine slacks, neatly pressed.

"Kiss me," Lila lifted her head. "Don't ask questions."

"You funny one," Waldo breathed.

Lila grabbed her hair.

"You're mussing my hair."

"Yes, yes, yes," Lila said, rubbing with her hands and holding the scalp as though certain she must never let go.

She felt the movement of Waldo's lips against the side of her nose and down along one cheek, grazing past her lips to settle into the hollow of her throat.

Lila stretched herself upward, meeting the expanse of Waldo's hulk with her breasts, her belly. She circled the woman's waist with stiff arms, pulling her in closer, closer, drinking the flesh of her with every nerve, every pore of her body.

"Undress me," Lila whispered.

"But I just got…"

Lila stopped the words with her mouth. She didn't want to hear now, didn't want to know. Her fingers moved to open the buttons of Waldo's shirt and pulled it aside.

"Crissakes…" Waldo whispered incredulously.

Lila pulled her down to the floor.

"At least on the cot," Waldo laughed and lifting the small weight of Lila, put them both on the narrow mattress.

"Take me, baby," Lila whispered. "Just take me."

She felt Waldo's body coming alive, warming to the squirm and arching of her own flesh, firing up the coals of her need and glowing softly, to leap at any instant with her into the flames of desire.

Waldo's huge hands opened Lila's belt and pulled down the dungarees and searched beneath the curve of Lila's stomach.

"Easy," Waldo murmured as Lila reached to bite her shoulder. "Easy does it, honey. We've got all night."

"Don't call me honey," Lila blubbered.

Waldo's breath touched her eyelids. "Why shouldn't..."

"Just don't."

She tried to free herself of Waldo's embrace, wanting to be the aggressor and hold her own, possess her triumphantly, proclaim her need and her love.

But Waldo's body stiffened against this. "Who goosed you?"

And Lila answered, "Don't make fun."

They stopped making fun and began to make love in earnest. She could feel this in Waldo's sudden grim attentiveness, reaching over to conquer, to search out the intimate points of desire and fulfill each with the knowingness of mouth and tongue and caress.

Lila emptied and emptied the well of herself, forgetting the day, forgetting its harshness, believing only this golden truth of Waldo's attention, her love, her attunement.

She felt the touch of Waldo indelibly branded on her brain, on her flesh, through her insides. And if she lived to be a hundred, Lila knew that this moment would always live for her with the burning clarity that she felt now.

They lay awake long into the night, talking idly about the show and the people. Small in the curve of Waldo's arm, she could hardly remember all the cruelties. She could forgive Marge her cynicism. She could certainly forgive Waldo for lending Marge the car.

"I didn't know you owned another pair of trousers," Lila said with a soft amusement.

"Oh, you don't know lots of things," Waldo murmured against her ear.

Lila agreed.

"I'll pay the electric bill tomorrow," Lila said, her mind jumping from one responsibility to another. "Then I'll never miss you again."

"Like ships that pass in the night?"

"Don't be corny."

"I will if I want to."

Lila suddenly tightened her embrace. "You'll keep all your clothes here from now on, won't you?"

"It's inconvenient."

"Why? I can wash and iron with the best."

"All right then, if that's what you want."

"You know what I want. I've told you a million times."

Waldo sighed. "I just don't like to make you a...a domestic."

"You goof," Lila grinned in the darkness. "Every woman likes to take care of her ..."

"... husband?" Waldo completed the sentence.

Lila felt her cheeks begin to burn.

"Don't let it embarrass you," Waldo said gently. "I know you've been married."

"Do you? I didn't tell you."

"But you did, honey."

"How?"

Waldo chuckled. "Lila, don't be silly," she said. "Your body gives it away."

"No."

"But yes. The way ... the way you want it. The way you like it. Very heterosexual of you, my dear."

"Don't be coarse."

"I'm being honest." Waldo lifted herself on one elbow and stared down at Lila. "Why are you afraid to face the truth?"

Stunned, Lila could only splutter. "I only know that I love you, Waldo."

"That's your romantic soul. After all, how could you help it? I look like I need a mother, don't I? Don't you want to take care of me? You know, the way your heart goes out to Allen."

"Waldo, stop this. It's insane." Quickly, she cast about for some words to reassure, to convince this woman of her total yielding to their relationship. "If I wanted to be a mother, I'd go home and make my own babies."

"How come you never have?"

Lila pulled away. Waldo, never before concerned about her past, was probing too deeply. She felt off balance. Revealed to disadvantage. But she couldn't tell why.

"You only like trouble," Lila said. "That's what it is. You thrive on trouble and complications. I'm a very simple person. I want to love you and devote myself to your welfare. Why can't you accept it and believe in it?"

"On faith?"

"Yes."

"Because you're so damned nervous all the time. Chasing me here. Chasing me there. I begin to wonder, Lila. Are you running after me or away from yourself?"

Lila swallowed the sting of hot tears. She was beating her head against a brick wall even thicker than Danny's. What could she do, short of killing herself, that would prove to Waldo the feelings consuming her?

"I don't know what to say to you," she answered.

"Then don't say anything," Waldo paused. "Besides, you think I don't trust you, but I do. With who else would I leave the pictures, honey? Aren't you going to be in charge of them, and of my career, for the whole two weeks or so that I'm gone?"

"I suppose so," Lila admitted, subdued by this first touch of flattery.

"So behave yourself," Waldo yawned, "and go to sleep."

Lila moved aside so Waldo could stretch out. She felt far, far from any thought of sleep as she watched the quiet body at rest beside her.

What, after all, could she pluck of hope from their conversation? For Waldo's sweet words were like an ointment spread carefully over the wound. A wound that would grow and fester, Lila felt sure, because Waldo must leave her alone for two weeks and devote herself to Whitey.

Two weeks. The idea stabbed at Lila already as she felt the first spreading ache of loneliness. Two weeks in this drab room. Two weeks of Marge, of Jingle, of who knew what. For it was true, and Lila knew in her heart that it was true, that Waldo could be gone and returned by Monday night.

If she really wanted.

CHAPTER FIFTEEN

LILA dozed fitfully through the night, counting her scattered and sparse blessings in between sleep.

In Waldo's absence, she would have time and peace to furnish the loft. Make it liveable and presentable. She could get to know the various galleries around town. She might even meet some people who could really help—people like Whitey to substitute for such dubious friends as Marge. Then, she might also search for a part time job, put to use the typing and steno Danny had insisted she learn for emergencies.

And this was certainly an emergency, Lila told herself wryly as she crept from the cot to pace restlessly over the wooden floor. Separation would strain every fiber of their bond. No use kidding herself, Waldo was the forgetful type. In Provincetown, she might meet somebody new. Somebody with offers, somebody with glamour.

Well, she would just have to take that chance. Lila shuddered in the snappy breeze whirling up from the street. If Waldo really couldn't be trusted, better to find it out soon. Better to suffer the consequences before they could overwhelm her.

And yet ...

A strange stirring of discontent made Lila turn off the direction of her thoughts before she reached the truth that she knew, instinctively, she was unable to face.

With a blanket pulled tight over her shoulders, she sat cross-legged on the floor and waited for daylight, marvelling how Waldo could sleep so peacefully with turmoil eddying so close.

"Breakfast?" Waldo said as she opened her eyes.

"What am I supposed to cook for you?" Lila answered distantly. "Dust?"

She watched Waldo duck her head and pull the pillow tight around her ears.

"Come on," Lila said, shaking her. "We can get you one of your favorite sandwiches."

"Sick of sandwiches," Waldo grumbled.

Lila bent over and kissed the back of her neck. "That's a blessing." she laughed.

Waldo bounced up, lifting Lila with her and toppling her backward onto the couch. "We'll have fried chicken with maple syrup and waffles."

Lila laughed, returning Waldo's happy mood. "Just scrambled eggs for me, thanks," she said. "I'm the cowardly type."

"No adventure in your soul," Waldo nuzzled her throat.

"None, my friend. None at all."

They tumbled playfully, rolling like bear cubs, hugging, legs entwined.

"Why do I feel so good today?" Waldo chuckled.

"Because you're leaving town, I guess," Lila answered bluntly. "Who wouldn't feel good," she continued, softening the accusation, "to be escaping the mob?"

"Nonsense," Waldo answered with certainty. "I feel good because I have you."

"It should only be," Lila whispered, half to herself.

"Come on." Waldo pulled her up. "We'll have our farewell breakfast and you can think of me all week long while you're burping."

"No doubt," Lila smiled.

They dressed and scampered out into the sunshine, blinking up at a sky not as clear as it might be. Flags of gray cloud marred the sun and blew up gusts of wind. Wind that hinted of rain.

"What do I do with the pictures," Lila asked, "if it starts to drizzle?"

"Bring them in, of course," Waldo said, tilting her head with a grimace. "What'd you think?"

Despite herself, Lila hoped for the rain and for the time it would give her to push through her plans for decorating.

"Here we go," Waldo said, pulling Lila into a restaurant.

They ate lavishly, Waldo crowding the table with a variety of side orders that dazzled belief. Lila considered when the day would come that Waldo would start getting fat. She could picture her with a paunch swelling the front of her trousers. Not so gorgeous then. Not so hypnotically virile. For virile she certainly was now. Even in the fresh clothes and the dandified hair-do to make herself more acceptable to Whitey and Whitey's friends. If only Waldo had the guts to go to Whitey looking comfortable and slightly sloppy. Then this premonition would not plague her, this discomfort would not be lumped in her stomach along with the food.

"Well," Lila said at last, glancing up at a diamond shaped clock without numerals, "I'd better get your pictures on the road." Lila heard her own voice saying goodbye. Saying, have a good trip, darling. Saying, please come back to me soon.

Waldo heard it, too, and tried to glance in under Lila's eyelashes, fluttering down to her napkin.

"Now, you be a good girl," Waldo said to her gently, "and don't take any wooden nickles."

"How are you going," Lila asked, needing to prolong things just one more moment, "if I have the wagon?"

"I'm taking the wagon," Waldo explained. "You'll be storing the pictures in Chet's panel truck."

"Who's Chet?"

"The fellow next to us at the show."

"You know him?"

"Yeah. We met on line for the licences. I kind of explained things to him and gave him a few bucks ..."

"You take care of everything, don't you?" Lila said, suddenly cold.

"In my way."

Round and round and round ... Lila felt herself floating outward in concentric circles. Waldo thought of everything, knew everybody. Then why wasn't she successful by now? How was it that she hadn't yet finagled her way to fame and fortune? She was no youngster. Thirty five at least. Where had the years gone? What was defeating her?

Lila, who admired efficiency, had none of the answers.

But she didn't need answers now, she needed fortitude. In Waldo's absence, there would be plenty of time to think, to analyze, to plan. But for the moment, she must be cool.

Waldo said, "I have to get the car keys from Marge," ending Lila's thoughts with the cold splash of inevitability.

Lila paid the check and touched Waldo's swinging hand, from time to time, as they strolled down the street. There would be no intimate goodbyes, of course. Nothing corny like that. Oh, no. Waldo would simply speed off into the horizon as if she was going for a container of milk.

"I'll wait for you here," Lila said at the station wagon. She felt no inclination to face Marge, to irritate herself by allowing Marge another opportunity for smirking. She did not want these last moments with Waldo to be tainted with trivialities.

"Good enough," Waldo said and trotted away.

Lila waited. The three minutes it should have taken stretched into fifteen. Waldo, the long winded. The undeniably complicated. She needed an efficiency expert to straighten out this sluggard part of her character.

But Waldo finally appeared, flipping the keys around the end of her forefinger.

"I'll set you up first," Waldo said, heading the car toward Fifth Avenue.

"And what about your clothes?" Lila chided, remembering Marge's talk about all the packing.

Waldo shrugged. "There isn't room back there for a toothbrush now. I'll come back for the valise later."

Lila made no answer. Whatever Waldo wanted to do, she would do, why bother trying to talk sense?

Lila let Waldo set up the pictures and put herself into the chair, regretting that she had not remembered to fortify herself with reading matter as Chet had suggested.

"Hi," she called to him, feeling that she ought to start making friends with him so long as she would be using his truck.

Chet nodded, shivering a little into his bulky sweater. He did not seem willing to talk at the moment and Lila wondered how long he'd been sitting here and what comments he had been forced to take already, so early in the day.

"I guess that does it," Waldo said, wiping her hands carefully on a handkerchief. "Don't forget to phone Jingle. He'll help you set 'em up."

"All right," Lila said, knowing she had no intention of calling Jingle. In Waldo's absence, she would have no time for these fringe friends. No need for the complications they could avalanche.

"If you pay the phone bill," Waldo said, "I'll phone you every night."

Lila nodded silently. So this was Waldo's way of parting. Still mercenary, still partly romantic. And still sure of herself.

"I'll do that," Lila said because she had to say something. "And I'll pay the electric bill, too," she added. "So there'll be a light shining when you get back."

"That's my girl," Waldo whispered, bending low and patting Lila on the cheek.

Nothing more.

Waldo turned and slipped between cars to hop into the plush leather seat. She looked all shining and raring to go. She kept her eyes straight ahead, focused on the opportunities waiting for her in Provincetown.

The car sped off and Waldo waved one hand through the open window. But she did not look back.

Lila watched her go, craning her neck till the crowding of other cars blocked her view.

Chet looked up from his magazine. He pushed the heavy glasses up a bit on the bony bridge of his nose.

"You want to get us something to drink today or shall I?"

Lila crossed her legs neatly and folded her hands in her lap, feeling an odd sensation of lassitude creeping up from her ankles. With Waldo gone, it seemed like pints of her blood had been drained away.

"You go, Chet," she said. "I just want to sit here and watch the world roll by."

The world, with its offerings and its jeers, could not really touch her, as though a thin, protective layer of porcelain were painted over her skin. Like a water repellant. Or, perhaps, a hurt repellant.

Still, it was utterly possible that the clouds would split wide open and drop down a savior, someone with a fat wad of bills in his pockets who would buy Waldo's pictures so that tomorrow's headlines would read, GENIUS DISCOVERED IN GREENWICH VILLAGE.

Genius?

Could Waldo be a genius?

Lila eyed the pictures for the zillionth time and heard in her brain the faint cackle of Danny's laughter.

Chet returned carrying two paper cups of something steaming. Lila sipped at hers, trying to discover in it a taste of coffee when its flavor actually reminded her of something she might have washed out last night's stockings in.

"Some bargain," she called to Chet, managing a smile of gratefulness nevertheless.

Yet by afternoon, with the wind flapping canvas nervously, a second container of the same brew tasted quite welcome. The skin along her belly prickled with cold and she could feel the rising of goose pimples over the backs of her arms.

Still, the world continued to roll by, moving along the stretch of a stage empty now of all significance.

Four hours had passed. Waldo was well on the way to Boston, zipping happily along a smooth highway, the radio blasting.

The sun died early.

Chet turned up the collar of his sweater. "Come on," he said. "I'll help you with those things."

They piled the pictures side by side at the curb and he brought the truck around.

Its brown rusted sides rattled as Chet bumped the canvasses into its innards.

"You sure toss those things around," Lila said, contrasting this with Waldo's extreme care.

"What the hell," Chet said with nonchalance. "It's all in fun, isn't it?"

"Don't you care?"

He squatted at the edge of the truck, lifting in Lila's chair. "The way I figure it is this. Painting is unimportant. Don't look at me like that. I mean it."

"Maybe for you it's unimportant," Lila protested.

"I'll bet it was unimportant even for the best artists who ever lived. Like writing or dancing or music. What are they but tools, anyhow? A way of recording what you live, that's all. If you don't live fully, how can you paint a great picture or write a great symphony?"

"You're way over my head," Lila laughed.

"Am I?" Chet persisted, lifting a lock of his sandy colored hair from over his glasses. "Any dope can learn technique. That's the least of it. But what good is all the technique in the world if you don't have anything to say with it?"

"Okay, I'm convinced," Lila said, fending him off.

"You don't want to hear it." He locked the back door. "I guess I don't blame you. It kind of narrows the field, when you think of it my way."

He was right. Lila knew that she didn't want to hear it. If she listened to Chet, she might have to consider her opinions of Waldo's life. And her opinions of this she already knew.

That was the hardest part. Facing up to her disapproval of Waldo's way of life.

"Now, I'm not great," Chet continued anyway, "because I'm too easily satisfied. Or too scared to try and discover what goes on in the world beyond my own academic preoccupations. I play chess and read books and go to the movies with the various campus cuties that happen to strike me. But I'm narrow. Too narrow."

"So you paint those wistful clowns."

"Yep. That's me looking outward, but afraid to see."

"I think you like the idea of being scared," Lila said, taking a light from his cigarette.

"It's comfortable," he said. "I suppose it's the only way I know."

Lila thought of Waldo and remembered how scared the girl had been in Whitey's presence.

"But scared people don't always know they're scared," she said.

"That's for sure. Want a lift home?"

She heard him start up the metallic, chattering motor.

"No, I want to walk. That's when I do my best thinking."

"See you tomorrow, then. Ten o'clock, if it doesn't rain."

The truck bounced away, leaving Lila with time, with a whole evening to do whatever she might, unimpeded by the necessity of digging up Waldo.

But it was too cold to do much walking. And she decided to go straight home. Face the projects that had to be started. And face a night of sleeping by herself in the hollow, echoing room. One, only, of many such nights.

And Lila realized that not only Chet, not only Waldo could be scared.

Welcome to the club, honey, she told herself... and laughed if off because she couldn't really laugh it off at all.

CHAPTER SIXTEEN

L ILA found Allen sitting in front of her closed door.

"You're never here anymore." Allen punched at the cowboy hat that perched on his knees.

"Sure I am," Lila said, opening the door and glad for his company. "Only you're asleep those times."

"Well, why are you home when I'm asleep and out when I'm awake?"

"That's the way it is sometimes." she surveyed the empty room, somehow dingy and disgustingly unkempt with bits of sandwich leavings and Waldo's smelly shirt, trousers and old sneakers.

"Momma said to bring you back for supper."

Lila heard the certainty of Allen's lie, yet it pleased her that someone wanted her around.

"I'll be up," Lila said. "But first I have to clean this place a little." She wondered how on earth she intended to do this without a broom, without any dust rags, without so much as a waste basket. "On second thought," she mused, "I'll come up with you now." Minnie could supply her with tools.

Allen bounced ahead of her as they climbed the stairs. "Castles don't have to be cleaned," he chirped.

"Oh, yes they do," Lila said, laughing. "Castles and palaces and everything. You'd be surprised."

Allen turned on the step, smirking at her lack of knowledge. "Palaces have servants."

"Do they?" Lila scooted him along, cupping his hard little behind in her two hands.

"Sure. The men wear white stockings and all the women curtsy when you go past."

"You've been watching too much television," Lila said, stepping into Minnie's place.

"So, I thought you got lost," Minnie said, testing the bottom of an iron with one moistened finger. "Or maybe you moved out already."

"Not quite," Lila smiled. "Can I borrow a broom from you?"

Minnie set the iron down on its stand and smoothed a wrinkled shirt front along the board.

"You're cleaning up?" she said.

Lila heard something in the question that smacked of too much knowledge.

"A little," she answered evasively and accepted a cracker that Allen pushed into her palm.

"That means Waldo isn't home," Minnie stated.

"You know too much," Lila tried to keep it light.

"What do I know?" Minnie sighed but made no movement to find the broom. "Every couple of weeks, Waldo runs away. Then the girl she leaves behind comes asking for a sweeper."

Lila swallowed hard, choking down the dry cracker. "Is that the way it goes?"

"That's the way it goes."

"Maybe this time you're wrong?"

"Maybe I am."

But Minnie couldn't look at her and Lila knew that the woman couldn't be convinced.

"It remains to be seen," Lila insisted, hanging on to her slipping foothold of courage.

"Meanwhile, you'll eat some supper with us? A good hot supper."

"I've got to get busy."

"Don't worry," Minnie answered, testing the iron again. "For cleaning up, there's always plenty of time."

Privately, Lila conceded that she needed people to talk to. That stirring up the dust in the empty loft wasn't exactly what the doctor would have ordered for her morale.

Allen turned on the television set and propped himself before its fuzzy picture, content in Lila's presence.

"My Isaac stays late at the factory tonight," Minnie said. "It's nice to have someone for company."

Lila knew that Minnie wanted her to feel she was doing her a favor by staying.

"You're a good person," Lila said. "Let me set the table."

"With pleasure," Minnie beamed.

Lila wasn't hungry. She felt that she would never be hungry again. At least, not till Waldo came back and proved Minnie wrong. But she stuffed down the mashed potatoes and the meatballs just for the privilege of being here, where life still flourished with the persistent tenacity of weeds.

And somehow, Minnie wormed it out of her. The aggravations of her life with Danny. The stifling beneath his thumb. The nights of lying alone in bed ... for she might as well have been alone, with Danny snoring at the far side of the mattress.

As she talked, Lila realized this was something she had needed to do. Purge herself of the poison. Retch it all out. If Marge had ever been a true friend, she might have been able to do this years ago.

Minnie listened without comment. Though nothing could have stopped Lila's flow and tumble of confession.

"You know what a tyrant is," Lila said. "You must know, from Europe."

"Do I know," Minnie shook her head in violent agreement. "What I know from tyrants you could never believe."

"Then you understand why I have to get a divorce."

113

"No." Minnie squeezed lemon into her tea. "That I don't understand."

"But of course you do." She put her crumpled paper napkin into a dish and scraped spilled sugar from the tablecloth into her palm, infected with Minnie's passion for housekeeping.

"This Danny of yours. You think he is a tyrant? Well, I'll tell you what I think." Minnie took in a deep breath, lifting her cushiony breasts with grandeur. "I think he is a man." She waggled a finger sideways to quiet Lila's objection. "Not like the American men in the movies. Oh, no. But a serious one. You think to work and to save is to be a tyrant?"

"He never loved me," Lila added for emphasis.

"Hoo hah, love."

"Why do you make fun of it?"

"Me? I'm the last one for making fun of love. But to recognize it, there's where the trouble lays. Love. Saint Valentine's Day. Christmas goodies. This is love?"

"I never asked for Christmas goodies." Lila poured more tea to warm her fingers around the tall glass. "I only wanted a little attention now and then. Some sign of acceptance. Does Isaac turn away from you every night?"

"My Isaac has a head full with troubles. If he didn't turn away from me, I'd begin to wonder."

"Come now."

"All right," Minnie conceded. "There are times, I admit it."

"Well, for me there were no times."

"Never?"

Lila met the polished glare of Minnie's shrewd observance. "Well, there were times, but so few I could almost count them.

"So I told you." Minnie settled back, satisfied.

"But that's not enough," Lila said without shame.

"Then do something about it," Minnie answered factually. "Throw away the perfumes and be a companion to your husband."

Lila's cheeks burned. All of her pulsed against this enemy across the table who wanted her to turn back the clock and face again the frustrations she had finally outgrown.

"No?" Minnie said, reading her thoughts.

"No," Lila said flatly.

Minnie let go a long sigh. "So take the broom from behind that curtain and go downstairs. Go. Clean up after that *meshuggeneh* Waldo and make believe you're living a life."

Wordlessly, Lila went for the broom.

Though Minnie could not agree, Lila felt glad that she had unburdened herself to a sympathetic ear. The pockets in her soul where Danny had still lurked felt all turned inside out now and aired.

"I appreciate what you've told me," Lila said, her voice trailing off with the hope that Minnie understood.

"Never mind appreciate," Minnie said. "When the light shines through, then we'll make a celebration. Allen, turn that thing off and get ready for bed. Poppa's coming any minute."

Carrying the broom, a dustpan and a bundle of rags that had been Isaac's old shirts, Lila returned to the loft.

She lit a couple of candles and peered around the room to decide where she should begin. Coming back to her responsibilities toward Waldo felt like returning after a long war. Talk about Danny still rang in her brain. She didn't hate him, couldn't hate him, for he had meant well even though he had acted so clumsily, so thoughtlessly.

But Danny belonged to the past.

He didn't fit anymore. After Waldo's caresses, the thought of Danny's beard against her skin was too repulsive even to imagine.

Waldo had lighted dormant, waiting embers. Waldo had fanned the flames high.

Danny was like dry bread in comparison.

Energetically, she moved the broom over the dirt filled cracks, banged into the molding. Minnie, conventional and unimaginative, could never understand the experience of a night spent loving Waldo. Woman with woman was against the commandment, after all. And Minnie, like Isaac, feared such disobedience.

It was a conceivable fear, Lila thought, smiling to herself in the flickering candlelight. Better to be afraid of holy spirits than of … of Whitey.

The dirt piled high, making Lila sneeze occasionally as she dumped and rolled it into a spread of newspaper.

When she looked out the window, hours later, Lila saw that it had begun to drizzle so that the streets gleamed beneath the funnels of lamplight. The sky, a pinkish gray, loomed heavy with its burden.

Well, tomorrow she would be free from the trap of picture sitting. Tomorrow, she could scout the stores for her first pieces of furniture. Tomorrow, she would begin to prove that Minnie could be wrong. She would make a home of such warmth, such love, that Waldo would really have to be a *meshuggeneh* ever to want to leave it again.

CHAPTER SEVENTEEN

LILA slept from sheer exhaustion, from a kind of recklessness because there was nothing to lose.

A drugged sleep without dreams, but washed with colors like a great, stained ocean, washed over her.

When she awoke, it snapped into her brain that this was Sunday, that the days of the week had gotten mixed up and lost since she'd met Waldo. That her plans for shopping would have to be postponed.

And what would she do instead?

It still rained. The room felt damp, the wood warped and swelling beneath her bare, cold feet as she padded to the window and pulled its heavy frame shut.

She could go to the movies again. Kill more time. How much time had she killed already, just living?

She wished she knew Chet's last name or his phone number but Waldo had left her no clue.

Was it raining in Provincetown?

She pulled on her dirty pants and Waldo's dirtier sweat shirt, needing protection from the weather because she must go out, get away from her thoughts and from the stagnation of these thoughts that moved always in circles.

The rain soothed her nerves as it played against her head. She felt part of the weather, damp and dismal with it. So different from the day she'd left Danny. Her hopes then? How childish they seemed now—filled with theories, with ideals. She had been running to a career, to independence.

And where was she going now?

To a coffee shop. To search for someone to talk to. Kill more time, drown the passing moments of her life that dragged so slowly while the years flew.

At twenty five, what had she accomplished? What could she expect from the next months that would make her proud?

She was swinging between Waldo and emptiness. Sailing like one of Chet's wistful clowns, expecting to fall flat at any moment and hear a hearty, resounding laugh from the audience.

What audience?

Her own conscience. She could feel the eyes of her conscience following her every move with Danny's critical eyes.

This will never do, Lila told herself. The rain interfering with her responsibilities to the show. And Sunday interfering with her plans for domestic bliss.

So she could blame circumstance and feel absolved. Tomorrow would be different. Tomorrow, a clean slate on which to write all the correct answers.

But now, coffee and company. She peered through a water smeared window, hoping to find Jingle somewhere in the crowd.

She saw Carmen instead. Carmen sitting alone, far back in one corner of the room, chin propped on the heels of her hands. Her round, ruddy face stared off into a private vision of the flames of hell. A face, grief stricken like the photo of a woman staring down at a burned out home, of sudden quick destruction that brought puzzled silence and a helpless lethargy of panic.

Lila thought that she ought probably to leave her alone. That Carmen must be waiting for Marge. That Marge was late, as Waldo could be late. That to intrude upon Carmen could be of no help to either of them.

Yet Lila's steps carried her inside, moving her irresistibly toward the one person who suffered feelings harmonious with her own. Carmen was in no position to give advice, as Minnie could.

Lila pushed around tables of chess players, other tables of argument and laughter. The rain had sent people inside, to form a little party of tiny, round tables. People united by the weather, by the community of Village life, unmatched for togetherness anywhere else in the city.

"Well, hello," Lila said, making it seem as though she had wandered to Carmen's table by accident.

"Hello, Lila." A cup of espresso stood untouched between her elbows.

"Care for some company?" Lila said, treading lightly.

Carmen smiled with a warm sadness that lit her puzzled eyes with a kind of new polish. "Of course," she said. "Good to see you."

Lila pulled out a chair and lowered her damp behind gingerly to the velvet cushion. "Crowded today, isn't it?" She spoke impersonally, not wanting to poke Carmen where it might hurt.

"I guess it is," Carmen said, rousing a little. She turned the handle of her cup, lifted it to her pale lips, then lowered it without tasting it. "What've you been doing lately?"

"Nothing much," Lila said, crossing her legs and leaning against the wrought iron back of her chair. "Sweeping out the house. Thinking about the show. It's a lousy time. I don't know where people get off, coming down to look at the paintings and being so stupidly critical."

"I didn't know you painted," Carmen said, trying to muster interest.

"But I don't," Lila smiled. "Waldo's paintings."

"You're sitting for Waldo?"

"Of course."

Carmen rustled a package of sugar and tore it open viciously. "Gosh, you're stubborn," she said.

The vehemence surprised Lila. It also gave her pause. She knew better than to ask the next question. Yet she couldn't keep it from happening.

"Why shouldn't I be?" she said in a low voice.

Carmen shook her head. Some frizzy hair fell across one shoulder. "Maybe you've got ideals," she said. "I haven't. Not any more, I haven't. I haven't got ideals or patience or anything good left in me."

"I wouldn't call it patience or ideals," Lila said, feeling herself running downhill and powerless to stop.

"You ought to, though. Because all I've got left is this terrible desire to kill. You know. To take a butcher knife and stab and stab and stab…"

"Nonsense."

"Yes. That's what Marge told me. That it was nonsense. That I was only feeling this way because it was all so new to me and that I'd get over it when my next lover came along. But there isn't going to be any next lover. And when I said that, she only laughed at me like I was an idiot and skipped out of the house with Waldo's valise. You'd think if they were so hot for each other, they'd be living together, wouldn't you?"

Lila felt the sudden jerk of panic inside the back of her neck. She glanced around for a waitress and ordered coffee before she lost all capability of speaking.

"Waldo went to Provincetown," Lila said like a prayer, "to see Miss White and make arrangements for the summer show."

Carmen wet her lips while she stirred the sugar round and round, clenching the tiny spoon till her fingernails went white.

"Is that what she told you?"

"That's where she went," Lila insisted. "You were there when they arranged it."

"I was there, all right," Carmen choked. "I was there for lots of things."

"Like what?"

"You don't know? You don't know any of it?"

"All I know," Lila insisted blindly, "is that my Waldo went to Provincetown."

Carmen's shoulders sagged. "I'm sorry," she murmured.

"But it's true."

The waitress brought Lila's coffee and slapped the check beside the ashtray.

"Isn't it true?" Lila said when the girl left.

"Oh, they went to Provincetown, all right."

"They?"

"Don't be so stubborn, Lila. You know what I'm saying. Why do I have to put it into words?"

"Because I don't believe it. I won't even believe it if you say so, Carmen."

"You'll have to believe it," Carmen quavered. "Because I saw it myself. The two of them. Marge and your Waldo together in that nice, new, shiny wagon. And maybe they did go off to Provincetown. But Marge told me not to be in the apartment when she got back, so I naturally assumed…"

Lila met Carmen's questioning eyes. "I'm sorry," she said at last. "I really am sorry about it for you." Impulsively, she reached around the table and touched Carmen's thigh. "And even if it does sound callous, you will get over this. People just go right on living, that's all."

"But I loved her," Carmen said softly. "I gave up my whole life for her. I worked and I did her clothes and I entertained her friends and…" She rattled off the meaningless list of things that should have promised her the reward of Marge, but didn't.

"Who knows?" Lila said, for the girl needed something to soften the blow. "Maybe she'll change her mind and come back. You did all those things for her and I know she must miss you."

"Marge wouldn't miss the hair out of her armpits," Carmen said with a quick bitterness.

"Look, you come stay at our place til you make up your mind what you want to do, Carmen."

Carmen shook her head. "So you won't believe me?"

Lila didn't answer. What could she say? How could she tell Carmen that Waldo was somehow different? That Waldo would have to come back? That her life and Waldo's were too entwined with faith and trust? To Carmen, it would sound like foolishness.

And maybe it was foolishness.

Yet, if she gave in, if she accepted this story second hand from Carmen, she wouldn't deserve anything better than Waldo's disloyalty.

No, she dared not believe this girl's story. Perhaps Marge did go with Waldo to Provincetown. Certainly, Marge didn't love Carmen...this had been obvious from the beginning. But for Marge and for Carmen, it was different.

Lila swallowed the icy dread along with the steaming coffee, shutting her mind with a kind of desperation to the possibility that Carmen's story could be anywhere near accurate.

They stayed and they talked about other things, the little things that people while away time with, the incidents that serve to relieve the eye by distracting it from some horrible sight.

Lila drank lots of coffee and ate some kind of heavy white cheese, as though by stuffing herself, she could prove her nonchalance in the face of Carmen's tale of disaster.

The rain grew heavier, pounding thickly in slashes, making trickles down the window pane that showed the world outside in a blurred and distorted image.

Thunder rolled far off and then the rain gradually lessened. Automobile lights flung their gaping eyes at them intrusively. People dared the rain by dashing across the street with soaked newspapers wilting over their heads.

"Come on," Lila urged. "We can't sit here all night." She made Carmen get up and hailed a taxi to take them home.

The reality of the loft seemed to tell Lila that Carmen's story had been a nightmare. Only a dream. A passing tale that would dissolve with the coming of Monday and the resumption of responsibilities.

Only idleness had allowed her imagination to run away with itself, puffing up a meaningless thing into something grotesque.

No, Waldo's love could not disappear over the horizon this quickly.

Lila lit a candle and set it to glimmer on the windowsill.

"I must pay that damned electric bill tomorrow," she said, supporting herself with this very immediate project. "And the phone bill, too," she added hopefully.

Carmen sat limply on the cot, her feet pigeon toed like a puppet with its strings cut.

"Now, you forget everything and go to sleep," Lila said, putting on airs like Minnie. "I have lists to make."

She got Carmen undressed and into bed, safely tucked down for the night.

Then she turned her back on this silent grief that she could not help and went to stare at the drizzle falling silently, watering the ground where no flowers could grow.

Her brain, so sharp, so sure just a few hours ago, had begun to fall apart at its seams. She had spoken so bravely of trust. So certainly of faith.

But alone now with her thoughts, she felt the courage fly, like geese winging away, leaving behind only the derisive echo of their cry.

CHAPTER EIGHTEEN

FACING Carmen in the morning was like gazing at the reflection of herself in a broken mirror.

"I've got to get to the show," Lila said, calling up all the discipline she could command.

Briskly she washed her face, combed the straggled ends of her hair that needed to be trimmed and put on lots of make-up.

Paint on a smile, she thought. Nothing to be gained by falling apart. And she counted on the variious duties of the day to support her, to see her through.

"I've got to be going anyway," Carmen said helpfully. "Better clear my things out before Marge gets back. If she ever does."

And so they parted, friends who would never meet again, drawn together by a moment of shared unhappiness, to go their separate ways and find … What?

Lila couldn't think about it now. Stubbornly, she held in mind the needs of the moment. Peel one potato at a time, work down gradually to the bottom of the pile.

The clearing day glimmered with strengthening sunshine. Monday. Back to the office, back to school, the city came grumbling alive, floating streams of people to subways and buses. New shoots of tender grass had pushed up overnight, lighting the seeded dark earth with fresh color. Lila strolled through the park for a while, gaining balance, struggling for perspective as she gave herself to the cycle of death and regeneration clamoring to be heard even here in the artifice called civilization.

When she reached her place on Fifth Avenue, Lila saw that Chet had already set out the pictures.

"Have a good weekend?" he said.

"Not bad," Lila said, brushing away all contemplation.

She settled down in her chair to wait. But the crowds of Saturday did not come now. Occasional strollers, Villagers mainly, paused, then passed on, accustomed to the show and empty of comment.

Restlessness prodded, thorny and insistent.

"Look," she said, after two hours of fighting it. "Could you be sweet and keep an eye on things for me, Chet? I've got bills to pay that won't wait." She was thinking of the phone call tonight. Waldo's promised phone call. The voice over miles of thin wire that would end her worries, prove Carmen's verdict false.

"Sure," Chet called. "Go ahead. I'm more used to this than you are anyway."

"I'll bring back supplies," she said lightly. "How about some shrimp in lobster sauce?"

"A pizza with anchovies would be much appreciated," he grinned.

"Sold," Lila answered cheerily and hurried away to travel uptown to pay bills.

In the mass clattering of typewriters and violet hued efficiency of fluorescent lighting, Lila wrote checks.

A man's best friend is his money, she thought without cynicism, grateful that she had the cash to alleviate her distress. A mild application of dollars to the wound. In her heart, she thanked Danny for having been no spendthrift.

Back at the show, she sat out her sentry duty, glad to watch Chet enjoying the pizza. She read his magazines, hoping to concentrate on something other than herself for a change. He brought ice cream from the Good Humor cart. The afternoon spread and closed again into a fist of darkness. They stacked the pictures and Lila went back to the loft.

To wait.

She stared at the phone and circled round it. It lay silent on the floor, silent like an impudent child.

Ring, damn you.

And Lila cursed the phone because it was less painful than cursing Waldo.

She knew she ought to bring some groceries up to Minnie to balance up the dinners she had eaten there. But she couldn't leave. Couldn't part from the phone, in case it might ring in her absence.

Trapped with the pictures by day…trapped with the telephone by night.

Forgetting to snap on the lights, she sat among the shadows, entrenched in the habit of feeble candlelight and silence and bareness of walls rising blank and cold and unwelcoming.

For a while she sat on the windowsill, gazing down at the knots of men gathered in the good weather. Some women pushed baby carriages. Boys pitched pennies, crouching with enthusiasm and concentration.

Morning came round again, crowding against Lila's imaginings of a gleaming station wagon overturned on the road, smashed up, bursting into flames.

Eventually, she ambled back to the show, her feet dragging with the shackles of horror and entrapment.

She flopped into the chair, the marrow of her bones quivering like jelly from lack of sleep, from the exhaustion of nerves. Lila closed her eyes and tilted her face to the sun, warming and feeding from its benevolence. Her thoughts mingled and grew hazy.

"So this is how the free woman spends her time, is it?"

The voice jolted Lila awake. Her burning eyelids blinked open. A headache knifed across her forehead.

"Danny," she croaked.

An instinctive desire to run from him exploded, then died. She tried to smile, to hide her true feelings, to be cheerful and debonair and recklessly happy... to imitate Waldo. The attempt fizzled and Lila merely looked away from him, wishing Danny invisible, wishing herself into dust so that he could not probe and find her unhappiness.

"You come to the Village a lot these days," she said, to keep the conversation off herself. "What, may I ask, is it doing for you?"

"It's springtime," he said, rolling up his shirt sleeves with his usual neatness. "Good place to walk. We used to walk here, Lila."

"You always hated it," she said flatly.

"What I hated," he said, "was that dank place where you lived. And anyway," he grinned, "I knew I'd run into you sooner or later if I just kept coming back."

"You don't want that," Lila said, lighting a cigarette. "You don't want to know me anymore. I guarantee it."

"I'm a stubborn man."

"Not half as stubborn as I am."

Danny took out a pipe and filled it from a new oilskin pouch. "Who belongs to those paintings?" he said, veering away from argument.

"A friend."

That was a simple way of putting it, Lila thought, congratulating herself. A friend... a casual so-and-so. Nobody important.

"None of your old cronies painted," Danny mused. "Must be somebody new."

Lila nodded, afraid that if she answered, her voice might crack and give the whole thing away.

"Not bad," Danny said. "Undisciplined, but the brush work'll hold up."

"Thanks," Lila said acidly. "You want to buy one?"

Danny chuckled. "I'm pretty broke," he said honestly.

It was a punch below the belt, yet Lila knew that Danny hadn't meant to hurt her.

"Then you're no good to me," Lila retaliated with automatic defense.

She saw him raise one eyebrow and observe her in that detached manner of his that had always irritated.

"You never believe me," she blurted. "How could a person live with something like you?"

"I believe you when you're not playing games."

Something in her tightened, wanting to cry. Not with agony, as Carmen had cried. But with a strange relief. She suddenly could see herself through Danny's eyes, strutting across the stage, reading her lines, getting all concentrated and waiting for her cues. It was a game, really, all these complications, all the nonsense of drama and involvement. Real life could be painting, it could be living at random from day to day. But not for her. Not truthfully. Minnie ironing and preparing for Isaac's return at night … this was real. This she could understand. And toward this she had been struggling with Waldo.

Waldo … who saw none of it, who swung away from her on the opposite end of their seesaw of passion.

But pride in living could be separate from love. She could admire Minnie, yet what good was admiration without the warmth of the person you needed breathing close?

She gazed up at Danny now, feeling her eyes sunken hollow into the skeleton of her face.

"Come on," he said softly. "We've got to talk about this sometime. Why not now?"

Lila shook her head. She could feel the cracks in her stubbornness beginning to lengthen.

"If you really want a divorce," he said, "you can't be afraid of a little honesty."

Honesty? Yes, a little explanation would go a long way. If she told Danny about Waldo, his disgust would kill all hope for reconciliation. He would walk out and leave her in peace. Since privacy could not release his grip, honesty alone remained to do the trick.

"All right," Lila agreed, warming, almost eager to display herself for Danny's derision. If he had felt contempt for Marge, for the way she had been living when they met, how much more would he feel now for Waldo?

"Chet?"

Chet waved her on. Apparently he had been listening behind his magazine and wanted to help.

"We'll go home," Danny said, "where we can relax."

"Whatever you like."

They strolled to his Chevy, parked some blocks away.

Lila sat in silence as he drove, lacing together the fragments of all she would say, putting it mentally into some kind of order. For Danny, who had no use for wild emotions, must be shown the order, the inevitable trend and pull of her life away from his.

They rode up in the elevator in the clean, yet musty smell that had surrounded her old life like an embrace.

Danny took out the single key and flipped the door open.

She stepped inside, to the piles of text books stacked beside his desk.

"Sit down," he said, motioning to the Danish sofa they had purchased at a sale ... for cash. "Be my guest."

"How about some coffee?" Lila said, preparing herself.

"You don't usually drink coffee," he said with casualness. "I've got a couple of stale tea bags."

Despite herself, Lila smiled, recalling the old routine of her life, her preferences that Waldo had never bothered to discover. They weren't important, perhaps. But they were comforting.

"I'd like that," Lila admitted.

While Danny put up water in the kitchen, she stretched out, easing her body along the foam rubber. He wasn't pressuring her, she realized, not trying to overwhelm her with no-nonsense attitudes. The relief of this opened her mind a little, made room for her to collect and assemble the jagged bits of herself torn loose by Waldo.

Danny brought in a teak wood tray, an anniversary gift from his folks, with two cups and the white porcelain tea pot they had chosen together … how long ago?

"You were going to tell me about your friend," Danny said with gentleness.

Lila sipped her tea. "Maybe I need something to go with this," she said, stalling for time now, stalling the thunderbolts of Danny's disdain.

"Brandy?" he said. "You look like you could use some."

"Fine."

She drank the brandy fast. Then asked for more. For more courage to get her started.

"It's going to be a long story," she laughed, after her head had begun to swim a little. "And it starts with one word." She flung herself nonchalantly back against the pillows. "Sex."

Danny didn't comment.

She blinked across at him and watched him receding slightly into the drapes, drifting far away, mingling with the alcohol and with her sudden opening carelessness.

"Know what sex is?" she chided, hitting out at him. "No, you wouldn't, Danny. You wouldn't know about sex at all. You're the cold fish that sends out sperm cells once a year when the mating season comes around. Sure, what would you know about sex?" she blithered, her knees widening at recollections of Waldo.

"Please," his voice washed up to her from its great distance. "We're not ready to talk about me yet."

"Why not you? Weren't you the direct cause of my very, very sexy effect?" Lila giggled with wanton release. "Weren't you the guy who practically kicked me out of his bed so that I went tumbling downhill … All, all the way downhill, right into the arms of my precious, darling, wonderful Waldo?" Lila hiccoughed and took another sip of the brandy glittering with lamplight. "Waldo, my *meshuggeneh*. That means crazy, you know? And I'm a *meshuggeneh* too. Crazy in love. Crazy with desire. Oh, how I want to be kissed and held and … But you don't want to hear about such things, Danny. They probably bore you. Only, if you were a Lesbian, it wouldn't bore you at all. You'd probably be sitting right here, close up to me, whispering sweet nothings because you wanted to make love …"

"Is that it?"

"Women. Oh, women know how, I can tell you." She sucked in her breath, feeling a deliciousness roll through her. A delectable memory that brought with it the emptiness of pain. "Well, don't say I never told you that I needed it. Sex, that is."

"You need it now?"

"All the time, that's for sure. Yes, and right now, too. But not from you, Danny boy."

"I'm not as good as your Waldo …"

"My Waldo?" she said slowly. "Did I say that? Wish it were so. Heaven only knows who she belongs to, running away from me like that." She drained her fourth glassful of the brandy. "I've got to go to her, Danny. Got to see and touch her again. Got to find out if …"

Drunkenly, the story of Waldo's desertion sputtered from her lips, pouring like an open infection. Their days together, the nights, their misunderstandings, Carmen's story … all drained from her system.

"I can't just sit here and pretend everything's fine," Lila squeaked, "when I know it isn't, don't you see that? I've got to go there and stare Waldo in her lousy, beautiful face and make her tell me the truth for once. I just can't pretend any more. I need it black and white, like a ledger. I've got to know what the balance is … Got to know whether I owe her an apology or if she owes me. Debits and credits …"

"That I understand," Danny said. "It's what I'm doing with you, in a way. Debits and credits."

As she reached uncertainly for more brandy, he came over and took away the bottle.

"That's enough for a while," he said. "Better rest and pull yourself together."

"Why?" Lila trembled. "What have I got to rest for?"

Danny set things on the tray and started carrying them back to the kitchen. "For the long drive ahead of you," he said calmly. "That's what for. Only, handle that Chev of ours with care because I noticed the clutch beginning to slip this morning."

"You never let me drive it before," Lila said. "Except in emergencies."

"Well," Danny disappeared around the door frame, "this is an emergency, wouldn't you say?"

She heard him running water in the sink and sat quite still, rolling her swollen tongue around inside her mouth. Gradually, it began to sink into her brain what she meant to do.

And the prospect of facing Waldo, quite unaware ... of catching her either in innocence or guilt, would clinch things once and for all, wouldn't it?

Lila let the drowsiness engulf her now. Sleep and gather strength to face ... whatever she might find in Provincetown.

CHAPTER NINETEEN

A DEADLY, hospital calm sat weightily on Lila's eyelids as she urged Danny's badly sprung Chevy toward the highway. He had made her take a bath and change her clothes and swallow a couple of vitamin pills. Then he'd written out directions to Boston and from there to the Cape. The paper protruded from the sun visor above, flapping occasionally, urging her on.

She did not know what Danny thought about all this—of her turmoil and addiction. He'd kept his thoughts to himself for once, allowing her the freedom of her own feelings.

For once, he had behaved like a person of flesh and blood. Now, when it no longer mattered to her what Danny felt, he had conducted himself like a friend.

But thoughts of Danny flew as the car sped to the urging of her foot pressing down on the gas pedal. The dashboard clock, always half an hour slow, said three thirty. Trucks, but few cars, sped past, moving like phantoms in the martini glow of sulphur yellow lights. Her skin felt crisp and cool for the first time in weeks. Yet, though she had slept heavily, almost drugged, she did not feel revived. Her thoughts, her expectations of what Provincetown would reveal sent a rotting stench through her brain.

She had promised Danny that she would stop every two hours for coffee and something. Promised him that she would not arrive like a wild thing, distracted and distraught. That she would not yield up her advantage of steady nerves and thereby distort her meeting with Waldo.

Dutifully she pulled up to diners along the way, gulped black coffee but did not feel it burn her tongue. She dunked doughnuts and swallowed leaden bites of them. Her feelings had shifted into overdrive, humming steadily, somehow detached from the sensations of mortal flesh.

It was right that she should travel alone. Danny had been sensible enough, sympathetic enough not to offer his company. And as the hours ticked away, Lila reviewed her so short past with Waldo.

Had it really only been two weeks? The tenor of her feelings seemed to stretch backward and forward, encompassing eternity. Her love, like a rash, had sprung full blown overnight and she was affected to her very roots, committed. Radically changed. A whole lifetime with Danny could not change her so completely.

In Boston, again to fulfill part of her promise to him, Lila registered at a hotel and made herself lie down to sleep and replenish. It was mid morning and she drew the shades to block out the slant of sunlight. Day and night, shaken together and rolled out like a pair of dice.

She stretched diagonally on the cool sheets, easing her limbs from the jouncing rhythms of the car. A spiral of pain up one side of her back registered where a loose spring bulged through the cracked leather. Danny's old, faithful Chevy.

The first blossom of a smile turned up the corners of her mouth as she dozed off.

Some hours later, the pressure of Lila's anxiety goaded her awake. She sat up and shook her head clear, feeling with one toe for her shoes. Two and a half hours from now and she would be in Provincetown. So near ... so close. She resisted the temptation to phone Waldo at Whitey's place and announce her arrival.

Instead, she went to the dressing table and studied her face in the dust streaked mirror. From her purse she took out the implements of disguise, smoothing pan cake make-up over the smudged circles beneath her eyes and along the lines of tension that made tight scrolls around her mouth. Her hair, newly washed and fluffy, shone with a clean brilliance. She combed the bangs into light whisps over her forehead. Create the casual look, the devil-may-care attractiveness that Waldo must appreciate. Then she slipped into a fresh cotton dress. A pale pink suggesting springtime and ease and cheerfulness. The shirring swirled out from beneath her narrow waist and Lila sighed with a downhearted mixture of satisfaction and futility at this game... the game she must play, to impress Waldo.

Once more seated behind the steering wheel, she spurted away on the last leg of her journey. She would arrive with bells ringing and banners flying.

The winding road narrowed, curving along the water's edge that lapped calmly along miles of sandy beach. Dunes stood up steeply here and there, waving clumps of buff colored growth austere with the remains of a hard winter. Only the line of boulder, beaten and rough, spoke of mists and driving wind as it hunched stubborn and unbeaten, waiting for the coiling wash of sun glinting waves. Lila rolled down one window and inhaled the fresh, salt tang. Yes, this was Whitey's background, complimenting her lack of compromise, her persistence, her stern backbone, all intermingled with the promise of kindness.

She sped past the stubbles of weathered houses pointing the way from Truro outward to the curved finger of land jutting into the ocean.

Then the bleakness fell away and she rolled slowly along a narrow street, craning her neck for Whitey's address that she had jotted down in Boston.

She found the number and parked across the street from the whitewashed house, to stare at it with disbelief. Something inside her had expected this all to be a dream. That there would be no house, no Whitey, no searching for Waldo here. A dream from which she would awaken to find Waldo lying beside her, pressed close in the narrow cot.

But it was true.

The house balanced crookedly above many steps. Its shutters, freshly painted black, encased white curtained windows paneled with small, clean panes. Some bushes near the steps had begun to swell with the first green promise of buds. They led her eye to the door and its brass knocker, polished and gleaming almost white in the strong sun.

Lila sat for a while and smoked a cigarette, noting how her fingers trembled as she shaved off the ash. This wouldn't do. She must be calm. Flamboyant, almost … as if she were at a picnic.

Waldo, fancy meeting you here.

The grim lie of it all slapped her.

She swung herself from the car and slammed the door shut, telling the world, telling herself: ready or not, here I come … in this hide and seek game with Waldo.

Her ankles wobbled a little on the wooden steps but she lifted her chin far above such a mundane matter.

The knocker, inviting, friendly … what would it reveal?

She lifted, then let it fall. It thumped pleasantly.

"My dear," Whitey said, her bosomy chest heaving, "what a lovely surprise." She stepped back to reveal a small pair of early American chairs placed comfortably in the ample entrance on opposite sides of an oval hooked rug. "Do come in, please."

"Thank you," Lila said, responding to the smile with one of her own. "I hope I'm not interrupting…" She came inside, bringing along all the manners she had ever learned. For Waldo was a matter entirely separate from Whitey. And Whitey, she liked.

Window sills foliaged with potted plants captured the outdoors and the sunshine. Lila's glance roved over them and beyond to the curving stairway that led to the second floor. No signs of Waldo yet. Was she sleeping? Nursing a hangover, perhaps? Or already out with Marge to trot the dunes and revel in the patch of freedom between New York past and New York to come.

"I must say," Whitey clasped her ringed fingers in front of her silk dress, "how glad I am that my invitation did not pass unnoticed."

They sat in the living room, separated by an opened box of candy, a vase of cut flowers in shades of yellow. Hothouse flowers, Lila knew, for Whitey would be anxious for Spring.

"Where are your things?" Whitey said, the monocle swinging over her chest. "We must settle you instantly."

"I only brought myself," Lila said with a little laugh, "just for a short stay. You're a busy woman, I'm sure, and I wouldn't want to inconvenience you."

"Nonsense, child. I love company."

The face that beamed at her held nothing of the lechery she had seen on Waldo's. Yet she knew that Whitey felt the same way about women as Waldo did. Another time, she might enjoy it here. Yes, enjoy it tremendously. "You must know," she said, "why I've come."

"Must I?" Whitey smiled, lifting the box of chocolates toward her.

Lila took one and set it on a small porcelain plate beside her. "Anyway, you can guess," she stumbled on. "Since I'm not a painter … or any kind of an artist."

"Yes, I can guess," Whitey said, sighing a bit. "Still, it's a pleasure to see someone, for a change, who has no need of my … facilities."

Despite herself, Lila felt a flush of heat creeping upward from her throat.

"Where's Waldo?" she blurted suddenly.

Whitey studied the open, fragrant flowers. "Yes, that."

"Isn't she here?" Lila hurried on, leaning forward. "Didn't she get here at all?"

"Oh, never fear," Whitey said, allaying Lila with her tone.

"She said she'd call me but she didn't."

"I know."

"You do?"

"Don't look so surprised. It ages your face a trifle and a pretty thing like you doesn't want wrinkles prematurely."

"Please, tell me where she is," Lila said, ignoring her.

"Well, now," Whitey shifted in her seat and crossed her ankles, "that comes later."

Lila fell into silence.

"At four o'clock you may see her."

"Why? Is she in quarantine?"

"Of course not, child. You can go to her now, if you wish, but I wouldn't advise an intrusion."

"Let me take that chance," Lila said firmly. "I didn't travel all the way up from New York to have a tea party with her."

"Then you must take the consequences," Whitey said, setting a clean ash tray beneath Lila's trembling match.

She walked with Lila to the door and pointed up the street.

"It's like a wild goose chase," Lila breathed, remembering, however, to thank the woman as she dashed away.

Lila ran, stumbling uphill, catching her heel in a bit of broken pavement, pushing on, the calmness, her promises to Danny all forgotten. Her heart rocked and swayed against her ribs, bulging for breath. Wind played with her hair, tangling it, destroying the aura of dignity practiced these many hours.

Past the crooked houses she swept, all blurring to inconsequence. Then down, down the steep winding hill where she burst into a small gray shack perched on a triangular corner of earth.

"Waldo, why didn't you call me?" Lila flung herself blindly, with exploding rapture, into the bare arms that held brushes and palette.

She felt paint smear across her cheeks as Waldo tried to pull away.

"What the hell..."

Lila held on tight, lifting her mouth, insisting. "I was so frightened," she breathed.

The heavy palette banged to the floor.

"Did Whitey tell you where to find me?" Waldo clipped the words.

"I'd have wrung her neck if she hadn't," Lila murmured. "Take me in your arms. I can't stand it … not another minute."

She felt the arms encircling her with stiff reluctance.

"Can't you see what I'm doing?" Waldo said. "You might have waited. Didn't Whitey tell you not to interrupt?"

"What does it matter, darling? Just this once …"

She almost climbed up Waldo's body, pressing her breasts to Waldo's hard chest, burying herself in the odor of turpentine.

Then, just as suddenly, as though a light had snapped on in her brain, Lila stepped back.

"But you aren't glad to see me at all," she said curiously.

"Frankly?"

"How can that be?" Lila said, the bits of her falling away like broken up pieces of a jig saw puzzle.

Waldo wiped her forearm over her nose and bent to pick up the palette. Sun drifted down through the skylight to burnish her hair. The big, single room filled with canvases glowed, waiting. Waldo contemplated the interrupted picture leaning on its heavy easel.

"When I work," she said, "I work. And when I play, I play. Now, can't you see, is work time."

"Play? Do you call my feelings for you play?" Lila shrieked.

Waldo sighed and stirred brushes in a jar. "I'm sorry," she said, "but this is something you'll have to learn."

"You might have called," Lila said for something to say. "Then I wouldn't have worried about you and you could be working to your heart's content. Think I don't want you to work, darling?"

"But how can I call when the phone is disconnected?"

Lila, stunned, had no answer.

"You had all that time to get the bill paid but you didn't," Waldo pressed her advantage.

"I paid it," Lila said, catching her breath. "I did my part. Did you? Did you even try to call?"

Waldo shrugged. "How was I supposed to know?"

"Faith," Lila said. "If you had only tried to call..."

"Like the time you went looking for me at Marge's place? Was that faith?"

It was true, what Waldo said. And yet it was a lie. Something rang false to Lila's ears, but she couldn't grasp exactly what.

"Like ships that pass in the night," she said with a crooked smile.

"Something like that."

She waited now for Waldo to make it better. For Waldo to laugh, as only she could, and dissolve their misunderstanding, make it tiny in comparison with what they felt for each other.

"Perhaps it would have been better if you had told me back in New York, the way Marge told Carmen, that it was finished between us." She held back tears, finding no use for them in the great, empty hall of her heart.

"I didn't say it was finished now," Waldo said. "Why the hell must you jump to such conclusions?"

"Because you don't love me. And that's the real truth, isn't it, Waldo?"

Waldo picked up a large rag, dipped it into turpentine and wiped her fingers slowly.

"No, not the truth. Far from it," she said, dropping the rag and coming toward Lila. "You're a real emotional type and that makes it hard on you. A person like me must be hard on anybody. But especially on somebody like you, poor little kitten."

And it happened now, as Lila had dreamed that it must happen. She felt Waldo's fingers spread across her back and lift her quickly close. The sharp cut of a tooth pressed her mouth open. A darting, seeking tongue found hers. Hands fumbled with the belt of her dress.

"Of course I love you," Waldo murmured, opening the buttons. "How could I love anyone else?"

Hot breath bathed Lila's eyelids. With a groan, she wiggled in closer, forming herself to the mold of Waldo's body.

They slipped together to the floor.

No questions now. No answers needed. Waldo opening her. Waldo seeking. Waldo probing and finding and taking...these were the answers. All that Lila needed.

"Hurt me," she muttered, wanting Waldo's love to destroy all the festering evil of her doubts.

"Oh, no, baby," Waldo crooned. "Not you. I wouldn't hurt you for the world."

Lila lay back and stretched her limbs, ready for the one source that could bring peace.

"Oh, yes, Waldo," she cried. "Let me live like this, baby. Always..."

Lila closed her eyes and yielded to Waldo thundering over her.

CHAPTER TWENTY

"ANYTHING you say, darling," Lila sighed. "You know that."

"Sure, when we're together, you get agreeable." Waldo, seated among the canvasses, drew deeply on a cigarette.

Lila straightened her seams. "Well, no more misunderstandings, that I promise you." She smiled slowly. "Besides, now that the phone is back, you have no more excuses."

"Then you'll be a good little girl and go home till I get there?"

"Of course. I'm happy to know you're here, safely working. What induced you to do it anyway?"

"I work here every summer," Waldo said. "Marge is up here, too, this year. It's sort of Whitey's gift to humanity."

"Well, you might have told me that before you ran off."

Waldo rubbed her head. "Who can keep track of all the things to tell you?" she said. "You're so damned particular."

"Efficient is the word. I like to know which direction is up."

"Agreed," Waldo smiled. "From now on," she poked a thumb into the air, "I'll keep you posted on every breath."

Lila didn't quite like the way she said it. Not the words themselves, but the tone. The strange feeling of incompleteness that she had known with Waldo...except when they made love...consumed her now and promised further misunderstandings. So soon? Would there never be an end to these complications, so unnecessary, that had no right to exist between them?

Faith. The old stand by.

"I'm going to do you a favor," Lila said blandly.

"Good. I could use one."

"No, I mean this."

Waldo leaned forward and kissed her on the knee. "What do you mean?"

"I'm going to walk out of here, just as though I never came in. You go back to your painting and at four o'clock, when you go back to Whitey's place, give her my regards and tell her I'm on my way back to New York."

For one hopeless instant, Lila wished Waldo to protest. But this, she realized at last, was impossible. Waldo, created not in the image of perfection, but in the image of her own strivings, grinned appreciatively.

"That's my good girl," she said.

Lila didn't look back.

As Waldo had sped away from her in New York, so now she hurried away to the car.

For two blocks she strode on, seeing nothing, hearing nothing, determined that no questions about Waldo's behavior would ever again come between them.

A gleaming fender jolted to a stop, just missing her as she plunged across the street without looking.

Reflexively, she glanced up.

There, smiling good naturedly, innocently, and slightly disconcerted by the near miss, was a face Lila had never seen before. A face behind the steering wheel of the Buick wagon.

Lila's jaw almost fell open. But then, why should it? Another face, another name, another complication. All part of the pattern of Waldo. And she had promised that there would be no questions.

She meant to keep that promise.

And she did keep it ... all the way back to New York.

For the questions, the many questions, would all be answered in time. The world was a small place and she knew she'd run into that face again. Sitting glumly in a bar, perhaps. Or in a coffee shop, as she had found Carmen. Just another of love's rejects.

Waldo's scalps. What else could they be? And they really didn't deserve questions at all.

She took the car back to Danny, parked it and delivered him the keys.

"That was fast," Danny said, his bare feet propped up on a coffee table.

"Thank you," she said.

"For what?"

"For not playing God."

There was no more talk to be made between them. Danny knew the score. He wouldn't be foolish enough to beat his head against her private brick wall.

Lila went to the five and dime and bought a tape measure to take back with her to the loft.

She measured distances and jotted them on a memo pad.

Projects to keep her afloat.

… A green carpet, dark enough not to show the dirt, washable. Two black leather chairs facing each other for comfortable talk. Scatter lamps for varieties of light, depending on Waldo's mood. A fold-away dinner table that could open for two or for six in case of celebrations. Stainless steel ware and pure white dishes. Some pussy willows in a long vase, just for kicks …

Waldo called. Waldo didn't call. There was no predicting.

But why worry?

She was beginning to get the hang of it now. Turn Waldo off when it bothered her. Snap her back on again in good moments. Simple, really, once you got in the stride of it.

Lila bought one of the paintings from the show and hung it on a wall, depositing its required price in a bank account for Waldo. Somebody had to buy them, after all. And she dared not count on Whitey.

As summer came on, Minnie's dinners grew even heavier. Lila took Allen to the movies where they could both bask in the air conditioning and the delights of days gone by.

One day without thinking about it, she called Cooper Union and arranged to take their entrance exams for the fall semester.

Jingle took her to the bars once in a while. And she played chess with Chet in his basement apartment.

All quiet, calm, dignified, efficient.

And sterile, Lila thought, as she closed her eyes night after night, alone on the narrow cot.

Danny called her once, but she turned him down.

"I'm being faithful," she said without shame.

"If it kills you?"

"Yes." And as she hung up the phone, Lila realized that this was quite possible, perhaps even likely.

The days took on a certain sameness, a mediocre quality somewhere between sleep and waking. She talked Minnie into going with her to the beach and she tumbled among the waves while Minnie sat beneath an umbrella, oiled like a chicken for roasting and knitting Isaac a sweater for the January cold.

"Aren't you a little early?" Lila said.

"So, for what should I wait?" Minnie answered.

And afterward, the question repeated itself over and over in Lila's brain.

For what should I wait?

... For Waldo's call, that came at last toward the end of August. For the voice, slightly hoarsened by sun and surf, eager to return to her and their life together.

And one afternoon, Lila hung out the window, popeyed and watchful for the Buick to come around the corner.

She knew Waldo would be late. That was part of Waldo's style and something she accepted after a whole summer of speaking to herself, of teaching herself patience and more patience.

Still, as she stretched breathless and expectant, all the months of loneliness, all the nights alone telescoped into a single night. A long night of gazing at the stars ... but of knowing.

And then she saw the car. Dustier than when she'd seen it last. One headlight battered in ... by that face, perhaps? Lila didn't know. She didn't care. She pressed her hands to her ears to keep her nervous brain from falling out of either side while the car slipped into a parking space and Waldo, still in the same sleeveless shirt, climbed out, went around back for some canvasses, then headed for the entrance.

Lila held her breath.

She turned to face the door, listening, alert, for the footsteps.

Her eagerness exploded simultaneously with the door bursting open.

"Hi," Waldo said, grinning, her skin dry and dark with suntan.

"Hi," Lila answered from the windowsill. And still she waited as Waldo dropped the pictures and stared slowly around her, face impassive in her usual expression of surprise.

"What's all this?" Waldo said slowly.

"Home," Lila said. And she beamed, proud of her accomplishment, glad that she hadn't given away her secret on the telephone.

And it looked like home to Lila, comfortable, the chairs slightly dimpled from her weight on them, the wastebasket filled with budget sheets that she had composed and finally discarded because she had no knowledge of Waldo's earnings, if any.

"Macy's?" Waldo said next.

"No, Sloane's, if you please. And B. Altman."

"Where'd you put the pictures?"

"I stored them with Chet. He has a back room."

"You cozy up with people pretty fast, don't you?" Waldo said.

Lila grinned. "Guess who taught me how." She winked, riding above Waldo's moment of disgruntlement. "How'd it go at the gallery?" she said to fill in the lull where Waldo's appreciation should have been.

"Fair. Come look."

Lila came forward as Waldo turned pictures for her to look at. "We made a sale at the show," she said casually.

"What?"

"Um hmm," Lila nodded to the wall.

"What the …"

"My money's as good as any, isn't it?"

"Oh, you goofy dope," Waldo said.

She let Waldo kiss her. The expected kiss, so long dreamed of. She felt the arms encircle her, as she had prayed for so long that they would.

"It's going to be all right," Waldo whispered against her ear. "You just wait."

Lila wanted to laugh. "What do you think I've been doing?" she said.

It echoed hollowly where her passion for Waldo should have been.

She let Waldo carry her to the studio couch and opened herself to the thrill, the old thrill that Waldo carried inside her like a secret amulet.

Lila felt the lips, hungry and eager, moving downward from her throat. "Kiss me," she whispered. "Make it yesterday."

Her body reached, begging for sensation. She tore at Waldo's shirt and pulled down the trousers, moving her mouth along the slightly perspired flesh, tasting salt, searching out her own need.

And then it came, like a crest of boiling ocean, bright, triumphant, roaring. She caught Waldo's legs with her own and clung, sifting herself, wheat with wheat, chaff with chaff, blending with all the good and all the bad of Waldo.

"Love me," she cried, as though impatient time would not stand still long enough.

"Little kitten," Waldo breathed.

Her mouth bruised Lila's flesh.

"You know I love you," Lila said, and repeating Danny's words, "even if it kills me."

"I thought about you all summer," Waldo murmured. "Every night in that damned barn of a studio."

I'll bet, Lila thought, remembering the face.

"Next summer we'll go together," Waldo said. "I can't be separated from you and make a go of it."

Running low on cash? Lila thought.

"You're so quiet, baby," Waldo said, stroking her. "What's running through that little head of yours?"

"Nothing," Lila said, feeling the lie of it. And the necessity.

They lay together, not pressed so close together on the couch as they had been on the cot. Comfortable, easy, conventional. Waldo, smiling up from the orange cushions, looked somehow washed out.

Lila, staring at her, realized that she had forgotten the color of Waldo's eyes and therefore had made a bad choice of colors.

"Know what we're going to do?" Waldo said, reaching up to kiss Lila on the chin.

"What are we going to do, Waldo?"

"Take a vacation together. Just you and me this time. No Whitey. No nobody. Just us." She groped for a cigarette. "I've been waiting for it."

"So have I," Lila answered.

Waldo lifted herself onto one elbow. "You don't seem quite right, honey. What is it?"

"Nothing," Lila answered. "Just nothing."

"Maybe it's me," Waldo put in. "I'm all painted out now and I guess everything looks tired. But you'll fix that, won't you?"

"Yes, I'll fix it," Lila answered.

Suddenly Waldo pulled her down and kissed her hard, searing her mouth, demanding.

And Lila answered the kiss, as she knew she must. When Waldo asked, she would answer. When Waldo needed, she would give.

They whirlpooled dizzily, coming up for air bright as porpoises, sinking and rising, convulsing at last in a final shaking off of desire.

And they smoked another cigarette.

"What we need," Waldo said, "is dinner. I want to take you out."

Out, Lila thought. Never home, but out … where the crowds are … and the faces …

"Good," she said gracefully. "Where would you like to go?"

Waldo swung from the couch. "Surprise," she said. "Kind of our own celebration."

"Celebrating what?" Lila asked mildly.

"Why, the reuniting of the world's nuttiest lovers."

"The *meshuggenehs?*"

"That's about it," Waldo grinned. "Besides, I want to tell you about my plans."

They dressed and went to the restaurant.

The right restaurant, with the right setting. With the expected candlelight flickering from emptied bottles of wine. With shish-ke-bob and exotic rice. Devastating.

But not real, Lila thought. Not something you could knit a sweater around, for January.

"… and with these new pictures," Waldo was saying, "Whitey thinks I'm about ready to make my bid for the exhibition in Chicago."

Quietly, Lila sipped her coffee.

"Only this time, you're coming with me. Like I said, honey, no more separations."

"That's nice," Lila said, wondering whom Jingle would rent the loft to in their absence. What lost little soul, eager for the gay life and just getting started.

After dinner, she went with Waldo to buy a bottle of Scotch.

"Just the two of us," Waldo winked as they came back to the lamp lights and the waiting chairs of their apartment.

They sat close together on the couch. Occasionally, she filled Waldo's glass, listening to the promises about Chicago. But if Whitey had said so, this time it would come true. This time, Waldo would be a success.

"It's going to be all right," Waldo mumbled, snuggling up against Lila's shoulder and closing her eyes.

Lila sat quite still until she was sure that Waldo had fallen asleep. Then she slid away from under her and lowered Waldo's head carefully to a pillow.

Yes, she would be a success, Lila thought. She had to be because there was nothing else in her life to distract her from it.

A success. Fame. Fortune. Glitter. The attention Waldo thrived on. And more work, which Waldo also thrived on.

She didn't pack anything. Not a toothbrush. Not a sock. She merely stood there for a long while and then because it was late and she might wake Allen, she tiptoed from the room and out of the house.

The streets smelled fresh with a first hint of autumn. She strolled across the park and listened to the secret, heavy leaves whispering among themselves.

The man with the skunk on a leash passed by. Lila bought an ice cream stick and licked at it slowly, glad for its touch of cold.

There was something about the promise of success that took a lot of waiting. More waiting, perhaps, than she had to give.

Do you live for the moment or don't you? Lila wondered.

And then the next question, the inevitable question, rocked her with its earthy truth.

So, for what should I wait?

She crossed through the park and came out on the other side, far from Waldo's loft, far from Waldo's expectations.

At the corner of Sixth Avenue and Eighth Street, she filed into the drugstore, hurrying a little because it was late and some folks liked to get to bed early.

In the phone booth, she dialled an old, familiar number. An uptown number, where today was every bit as important as tomorrow.

Danny answered in his usual detached voice, uncovering all the beauty she had never truly seen before.

And Lila said, "May I come home now?"

www.ingramcontent.com/pod-product-compliance
Lightning Source LLC
Chambersburg PA
CBHW052009240626
47153CB00008B/2805